# THE ENEMY STARS

In this superior novel of life and death in the farthest reaches of outer space, the reader is taken on a voyage which is at once an epic venture and a supreme testing of the human spirit.

With *The Enemy Stars*, Poul Anderson joins that small circle of science fiction writers who can project absorbingly the widest horizon of a limitless future and still not lose sight of men as individuals.

# The Enemy Stars

---

# Poul Anderson

CORONET BOOKS
Hodder Paperbacks Ltd., London

Copyright © 1958 by Street and Smith
Publications, Inc.
First published 1958 by J. B. Lippincott
Company, New York
Coronet edition 1972
Second impression 1973

This book first appeared in *Astounding
Science Fiction* magazine under the title
'We have Fed Our Sea.'

---

Printed and bound in Great Britain for
Coronet Books, Hodder Paperbacks Ltd,
St. Paul's House, Warwick Lane,
London, EC4P 4AH
By Hunt Barnard Printing Ltd.,
Aylesbury, Bucks.

ISBN 0 340 16480 8

# THE ENEMY STARS

THEY named her *Southern Cross* and launched her on the road whose end they would never see. Months afterwards she was moving at half the speed of light; if there was to be enough reaction mass for deceleration and maneuver, the blast must be terminated. And so the long silence came. For four and a half centuries, the ship was to fall.

They manned her by turns, and dreamed other ships, and launched them, and saw how a few of the shortest journeys ended. Then they died.

And other men came after them. Wars flamed up and burned out, the howling peoples dwelt in smashed cities and kindled their fires with books. Conquerors followed, and conquerors of those, an empire killed its mother aborning, a religion called men to strange hilltops, a new race and a new state bestrode the Earth. But still the ships fell upward through night, and always there were men to stand watch upon them. Sometimes the men wore peaked caps and comets, sometimes steel helmets, sometimes decorous gray cowls, eventually blue berets with winged stars; but always they watched the ships, and more and more often as the decades passed they brought their craft to new harbors.

After ten generations, the *Southern Cross* was not quite halfway to her own goal, though she was the farthest from Earth of any human work. She was showing a little wear, here a scratch, there a patch, and not all of the graffiti of bored and lonely men rubbed out by their successors. But those fields and particles which served her for eye, brain, nerve still swept heaven; each man at the end of his watch took a box of microplates with him as he made the hundred-light-year stride to Earth's Moon. Much of this was lost, or gathered dust, in the century when Earthmen were busy surviving. But there came a time when a patient electrically seeing machine ran through many such plates from many ships. And so it condemned certain people to death.

# 1

SUNDOWN burned across great waters. Far to the west, the clouds banked tall above New Zealand threw hot gold into the sky. In that direction, the sea was too bright to look upon. Eastward it faded through green and royal blue to night, where the first stars trod forth and trembled. There was just enough wind to ruffle the surface, send wavelets lapping against the hull of the ketch, flow down the idle mainsail and stir the girl's loosened pale hair.

Terangi Maclaren pointed north. 'The kelp beds are that way,' he drawled. 'Main source of the family income, y'know. They mutate, crossbreed, and get seaweed which furnishes all kinds of useful products. It's beyond me, thank the honorable ancestors. Bio-chemistry is an organised mess. I'll stick to something simple, like the degenerate nucleus.'

The girl giggled. 'And if it isn't degenerate, will you make it so?' she asked.

She was a technic like himself, of course; he would never have let a common on his boat, since a few machines were, in effect, a sizable crew. Her rank was higher than his, so high that no one in her family worked productively – whereas Maclaren was one of the few in his who did not. She was of a carefully selected mutant Burmese strain, with amber skin, exquisite small features, and greenish-blonde hair. Maclaren had been angling for weeks to get her alone like this. Not that General Feng, her drug-torpid null of a guardian, cared how much scandal she made, flying about the planet without so much as an amazon for chaperone. But she was more a creature of the Citadel and its hectic lights than of the sunset ocean.

Maclaren chuckled. 'I wasn't swearing at the nucleus,' he said. 'Degeneracy is a state of matter under certain extreme conditions. Not too well understood, even after three hundred years of quantum theory. But I wander, and I would rather wonder. At you, naturally.'

He padded barefoot across the deck and sat down by her. He was a tall man in his early thirties, slender, with wide shoulders and big hands, dark-haired and brown-skinned like all Oceanians; but there was an aquiline beak on the broad high-cheeked face, and some forgotten English ancestor looked out of hazel eyes. Like her, he wore merely an informal sarong and a few jewels.

'You're talking like a scholar, Terangi,' she said. It was not a compliment. There was a growing element in the richest families who found Confucius, Plato, Einstein, and the other classics a thundering bore.

'Oh, but I am one,' said Maclaren. 'You'd be amazed how parched and snuffy I can get. Why, as a student – '

'But you were the amateur swimwrestling champion!' she protested.

'True. I could also drink any two men under the table and knew every dive on Earth and the Moon. However, d'you imagine my father – bless his dreary collection of old-fashioned virtues – would have subsidised me all these years if I didn't bring some credit to the family? It's kudos, having an astrophysicist for a son. Even if I am a rather expensive astrophysicist.' He grinned through the gathering dusk. 'Every so often, when I'd been on a particularly outrageous binge, he would threaten to cut my allowance off. Then I'd have no choice but to come up with a new observation or a brilliant new theory, or at least a book.'

She snuggled a little closer. 'Is that why you are going out to space now?' she asked.

'Well, no,' said Maclaren. 'That's purely my own idea.

My notion of fun. I told you I was getting stuffy in my dotage.'

'We haven't seen you very often in the Citadel, the last few years,' she agreed. 'And you were so busy when you did show.'

'Politics, of a sort. The ship's course couldn't be changed without an order from a reluctant Exploration Authority, which meant bribing the right people, heading off the opposition, wheedling the Protector himself – d'you know, I discovered it was fun. I might even take up politics as a hobby, when I get back.'

'How long will you be gone?' she asked.

'Can't say for certain, but probably just a month. That ought to furnish me with enough material for several years of study. Might dash back to the ship at odd moments for the rest of my life, of course. It'll take up permanent residence around that star.'

'Couldn't you come home . . . every night?' she murmured.

'Don't tempt me,' he groaned. 'I can't. One month is the standard minimum watch on an interstellar vessel, barring emergencies. You see, every transmission uses up a Frank tube, which costs money.'

'Well,' she pouted, 'if you think so much of an old dead star – '

'You don't understand, your gorgeousness. This is the first chance anyone has ever had, in more than two centuries of space travel, to get a close look at a truly burned-out star. There was even some argument whether the class existed. Is the universe old enough for any sun to have used up its nuclear *and* gravitational energy? By the ancestors, it's conceivable this one is left over from some previous cycle of creation!'

He felt a stiffening in her body, as if she resented his talk of what she neither understood nor cared about. And for a moment he resented her. She didn't really care about this boat either, or him, or anything except her own lovely shell. . . . Why was he wasting time in the old worn

11

routines, when he should be studying and preparing – oh, hell, he knew precisely why.

And then her rigidity melted in a little shudder. He glanced at her, she was a shadow with a palely glowing mane, in the deep blue twilight. The last embers of sun were almost gone, and one star after another woke overhead, soon the sky would be crowded with their keenness.

Almost, she whispered: 'Where is this spaceship, now?'

A bit startled, he pointed at the first tracings of the Southern Cross. 'That way,' he said. 'She was originally bound for Alpha Crucis, and hasn't been diverted very far off that course. Since she's a good thirty parsecs out, we wouldn't notice the difference if we could see that far.'

'But we can't. Not ever. The light would take a hundred years, and I . . . we would all be dead – No!'

He soothed her, a most pleasant proceeding which became still more pleasant as the night went on. And they were on his yacht, which had borne his love from the first day he took the tiller, in a calm sea, with wine and small sandwiches, and she even asked him to play his guitar and sing. But somehow it was not the episode he had awaited. He kept thinking of this or that preparation: what had he overlooked, what could he expect to find at the black sun? Perhaps he was indeed under the subtle tooth of age, or of maturity if you wanted a euphemism, or perhaps the Southern Cross burned disturbingly bright overhead.

# 2

WINTER lay among the Outer Hebrides. Day was a sullen glimmer between two darknesses, often smothered in snow. When it did not fling itself upon the rocks and burst in freezing spume, the North Atlantic rolled in heavy and gnawing. There was no real horizon, leaden waves met leaden sky and misty leaden light hid the seam. 'Here there is neither land nor water nor air, but a kind of mixture of them,' wrote Pytheas.

The island was small. Once it had held a few fishermen, whose wives kept a sheep or two, but that was long ago. Now only one house remained, a stone cottage built centuries back and little changed. Down at the landing was a modern shelter for a sailboat, a family submarine and a battered aircar; but it was of gray plastic and fitted into the landscape like another boulder.

David Ryerson put down his own hired vehicle there, signaled the door to open, and rolled through. He had not been on Skula for half a decade: it touched him, in a way, how his hands remembered all the motions of steering into this place and how the dank interior was unaltered. As for his father – He bit back an inward fluttering, helped his bride from the car, and spread his cloak around them both as they stepped into the wind.

It howled in from the Pole, striking them so they reeled and Tamara's black locks broke free like torn banners. Ryerson thought he could almost hear the wind toning in the rock underfoot. Surely the blows of the sea did, crash after crash, through a bitter drift of flung scud. For a moment's primitive terror, he thought he

13

heard his father's God, whom he had denied, roar in the deep. He fought his way to the cottage and laid numbed fingers on the anachronism of a corroded bronze knocker.

Magnus Ryerson opened the door and waved them in. 'I'd not expected you yet,' he said, which was as close as he would ever come to an apology. When he shut out the wind, there was a quietness which gaped.

This main room, brick-floored, whitewashed, irregular and solid, centered about a fireplace where peat burned low and blue. The chief concessions to the century were a radiglobe and a stunning close-up photograph of the Sirian binary. One did not count the pilot's manuals or the stones and skins and gods brought from beyond the sky; after all, any one sea captain would have kept his Bowditch and his souvenirs. The walls were lined with books as well as microspools. Most of the full-size volumes were antique, for little was printed in English these days.

Magnus Ryerson stood leaning on a cane of no Terrestrial wood. He was a huge man, two meters tall in his youth and not greatly stooped now, with breadth and thickness to match. His nose jutted craggily from a leather skin, shoulder-length white hair, breast-length white beard. Under tangled brows, the eyes were small and frost-blue. He wore the archaic local dress, a knitted sweater and canvas trousers. It came as a shock to realise after several minutes that his right hand was artificial.

'Well,' he rumbled at last, in fluent Interhuman, 'so this is the bride. Tamara Suwito Ryerson, eh? Welcome, girl.' There was no great warmth in his tone.

She bent her face to folded hands. 'I greet you most humbly, honorable father.' She was Australian, a typical high-class common of that province, fine-boned, bronze-hued, with blue-black hair and oblique brown eyes; but her beauty was typical nowhere. She had dressed with becoming modesty in a long white gown and a hooded cloak, no ornaments save a wedding band with the Ryerson monogram on it.

14

Magnus looked away from her, to his son. 'Professor's daughter, did you say?' he murmured in English.

'Professor of symbolics,' said David. He made his answer a defiance by casting it in the Interhuman which his wife understood. 'We – Tamara and I – met at his home. I needed a background in symbolics to understand my own specialty and – '

'You explain too much,' said Magnus dryly. 'Sit.'

He lowered himself into a chair. After a moment, David followed. The son was just turned twenty years old, a slender boy of average height with light complexion, thin sharp features, yellow hair, and his father's blue eyes. He wore the tunic of a science graduate, with insignia of gravitics, self-consciously, but not so used to it that he would change for an ordinary civilian blouse.

Tamara made her way into the kitchen and began preparing tea. Magnus looked after her. 'Well-trained, anyhow,' he grunted in English. 'So I suppose her family is at least heathen, and not any of these latter-day atheists. That's somewhat.'

David felt the island years, alone with his widower father, return to roost heavy upon him. He stifled an anger and said, also in English: 'I couldn't have made any better match. Even from some swinish practical standpoint. Not without marrying into a technic family, and – Would you want me to do that? I'll gain technic rank on my own merits!'

'If you stay on Earth,' said Magnus. 'Who notices a colonial?'

'Who notices an Earthling, among ten billion others?' snapped David. 'On a new planet – on Rama – a man can be himself. These stupid hereditary distinctions won't even matter.'

'There is room enough right here,' said Magnus. 'As a boy you never used to complain Skula was crowded. On the contrary!'

'And I would settle down with some illiterate beefyfaced good Christian fishwife you picked for me and breed more servants for the Protectorate all my life!'

The words had come out before David thought. Now, in a kind of dismay, he waited for his father's reaction. This man had ordered him out into a winter gale, or supperless to bed, for fifteen years out of twenty. In theory the grown son was free of him, free of everyone save contractual overlords and whatever general had most recently seized the title of Protector. In practice it was not so easy. David knew with a chill that he would never have decided to emigrate without Tamara's unarrogant and unbendable will to stiffen his. He would probably never even have married her, without more than her father's consent, against the wish of his own – David gripped the worn arms of his chair.

Magnus sighed. He felt about after a pipe and tobacco pouch. 'I would have preferred you to maintain residence on Earth,' he said with a somehow shocking gentleness. 'By the time the quarantine on Washington 5584 has been lifted, I'll be dead.'

David locked his mouth. *You hoary old fraud,* he thought, *if you expect to hook me that way –*

'It's not as if you would be penned on one island all your days,' said Magnus. 'Why did I spend all I had saved to put my sons through the Academy? So they could be spacemen, as I was and my father and grandfather before me. Earth isn't a prison. The Earthman can go as far as the farthest ships have reached. It's the colonies are the hole. Once you go there to live, you never come back here.'

'Is there so much to come back to?' said David. Then, after a minute, trying clumsily for reconciliation: 'And father, I'm the last. Space ate them all. Radiation killed Tim, a meteor got Ned, Eric made a falling star all by himself, Ian just never returned from wherever it was. Don't you want to preserve our blood in me, at least?'

'So you mean to save your own life?'

'Now wait! You know how dangerous a new planet

16

can be. That's the reason for putting the initial settlers under thirty years of absolute quarantine. If you think I – '

'No,' said Magnus. 'No, you're no coward, Davy, when it comes to physical things. When you deal with people, though . . . I don't know what you're like. You don't yourself. Are you running away from man, as you've been trying to run from the Lord God Jehovah? Not so many folk on Rama as on Earth; no need to work both with and against them, as on a ship – Well.' He leaned forward, the pipe smoldering in his plastic hand. 'I want you to be a spaceman, aye, of course. I cannot dictate your choice. But if you would at least try it, once only, so you could honestly come back and tell me you're not born for stars and, and openness and a sky all around you – Do you understand? I could let you go to your damned planet then. Not before. I would never know, otherwise, how much I had let you cheat yourself.'

Silence fell between them. They heard the wind as it mourned under their eaves, and the remote snarling of the sea.

David said at last, slowly: 'So that's why you . . . yes. Did you give my name to Technic Maclaren for that dark star expedition?'

Magnus nodded. 'I heard from my friends in the Authority that Maclaren had gotten the *Cross* diverted from orbit. Some of them were mickle put out about it, too. After all, she was the first one sent directly toward a really remote goal, she is farther from Earth than any other ship has yet gotten, it was like breaking a tradition.' He shrugged. 'God knows when anyone will reach Alpha Crucis now. But I say Maclaren is right. Alpha may be an interesting triple star, but a truly cold sun means a deal more to science. At any rate, I did pull a few wires. Maclaren needs a gravitics man to help him take his data. The post is yours if you wish it.'

'I don't,' said David. 'How long would we be gone? A month, two months? A month from now I planned to be selecting my own estate on Rama.'

'Also, you've only been wed a few weeks. Oh, yes. I understand. But you can be sent to Rama as soon as you get back; there'll be several waves of migration. You will have space pay plus exploratory bonus, some valuable experience, and,' finished Magnus sardonically, 'my blessing. Otherwise you can get out of my house this minute.'

David hunched into his chair, as if facing an enemy. He heard Tamara move about, slow in the unfamiliar kitchen, surely more than a little frightened of this old barbarian. If he went to space, she would have to stay here, bound by a propriety which was one of the chains they had hoped to shed on Rama. It was a cheerless prospect for her, too.

And yet, thought David, the grim face before him had once turned skyward, on a spring night, telling him the names of the stars.

# 3

THE other man, Ohara, was good, third-degree black. But finally his alertness wavered. He moved in unwarily, and Seiichi Nakamura threw him with a foot sweep that drew approving hisses from the audience. Seeing his chance, Nakamura pounced, got control of Ohara from the waist down by sitting on him, and applied a strangle. Ohara tried to break it, but starving lungs betrayed him. He slapped the mat when he was just short of unconsciousness. Nakamura released him and squatted waiting. Presently Ohara rose. So did the winner. The retied their belts and bowed to each other. The abbot, who was refereeing, murmured a few words which ended the match. The contestants sat down, closed their eyes, and for a while the room held nothing but meditation.

Nakamura had progressed beyond enjoying victory for it own sake. He could still exult in the esthetics of a perfect maneuver; what a delightful toy the human body is, when you know how to throw eighty struggling kilos artistically through the air! But even that, he knew, was a spiritual weakness. Judo is more than a sport, it should be a means to an end: ideally, a physical form of meditation upon the principles of Zen.

He wondered if he would ever attain that height. Rebelliously, he wondered if anyone ever had, in actual practice, for more than a few moments anyhow. . . . It was an unworthy thought. A wearer of the black belt in the fifth degree should at least have ceased inwardly barking at his betters. And now enough of all the personal. It was only his mind reflecting the tension of the contest, and tension was always the enemy. His mathematical training led him to visualise fields of force, and the human soul as a differential quantity $dX$ (where $X$ was a function of no one knew how many variables) which applied just enough, vanishingly small increments of action so that the great fields slid over each other and – Was this a desirable analog? He must discuss it with the abbot some time; it seemed too precise to reflect reality. For now he had better meditate upon one of the traditional paradoxes: consider the noise made by two hands clapping, and then the noise made by *one* hand clapping.

The abbot spoke another word. The several contestants on the mat bowed to him, rose, and went to the showers. The audience, yellow-robed monks and a motley group of townspeople, left their cushions and mingled cheerfully.

When Nakamura came out, his gi rolled under one arm, his short thickset body clad in plain gray coveralls, he saw the abbot talking to Diomed Umfando, chief of the local Protectorate garrison. He waited until they noticed him. Then he bowed and sucked in his breath respectfully.

'Ah,' said the abbot. 'A most admirable performance tonight.'

'It was nothing, honorable sir,' said Nakamura.

'What did you . . . yes. Indeed. You are leaving tomorrow, are you not?'

'Yes, master. On the *Southern Cross*, the expedition to the dark star. It is uncertain how long I shall be away.' He laughed self-deprecatingly, as politeness required. 'It is always possible that one does not return. May I humbly ask the honorable abbot that –'

'Of course,' said the old man. 'Your wife and children shall always be under our protection, and your sons will be educated here if no better place can be found for them.' He smiled. 'But who can doubt that the best pilot on Sarai will return as a conqueror?'

They exchanged ritual compliments. Nakamura went

about saying goodbye to various other friends. As he
came to the door, he saw the tall blue-clad form of Captain Umfando. He bowed.

'I am walking back into town now,' said the officer,
almost apologetically. 'May I request the pleasure of your
company?'

'If this unworthy person can offer even a moment's
distraction to the noble captain.'

They left together. The dojo was part of the Buddhist
monastery, which stood two or three kilometers out of
the town called Susa. A road went through grain-fields,
an empty road now, for the spectators were still drinking
tea under the abbot's red roof. Nakamura and Umfando
walked in silence for a while; the captain's bodyguard
shouldered their rifles and followed unobtrusively.

Capella had long ago set. Its sixth planet, Il-Khan the
giant, was near full phase, a vast golden shield blazoned
with a hundred hues. Two other satellites, not much
smaller than this Earth-sized Sarai on which humans
dwelt, were visible. Only a few stars could shine through
all that light, low in the purple sky; the fields lay drowned
in amber radiance, Susa's lanterns looked feeble in the
distance. Meteor trails crisscrossed heaven, as if someone
wrote swift ideographs up there. On the left horizon, a
sudden mountain range climbed until its peaks burned
with snow. A moonbird was trilling, the fiddler insects
answered, a small wind rustled in the grain. Otherwise
only the scrunch of feet on gravel had voice.

'This is a lovely world,' murmured Nakamura.

Captain Umfando shrugged. Wryness touched his
ebony features. 'I could wish it were more sociable.'

'Believe me, sir, despite political differences, there is no
ill-will toward you or your men personally –'

'Oh, come now,' said the officer. 'I am not that naive.
Sarai may begin by disliking us purely as soldiers and tax
collectors for an Earth which will not let the ordinary
colonist even visit it. But such feelings soon envelop the
soldier himself. I've been jeered at, and mudballed by

21

children, even out of uniform.'

'It is most deplorable,' said Nakamura in distress. 'May I offer my apologies on behalf of my town?'

Umfando shrugged. 'I'm not certain that an apology is in order. I didn't have to make a career of the Protector's army. And Earth does exploit the colonies. There are euphemisms and excuses, but exploitation is what it amounts to.'

He thought for a moment, and asked with a near despair, 'But what else can Earth do?'

Nakamura said nothing. They walked on in silence for a while.

Umfando said at last, 'I wish to put a rude question.' When the flat face beside him showed no reluctance, he plowed ahead. 'Let us not waste time on modesty. You know you're one of the finest pilots in the Guild; any Capellan System pilot is – he has to be! – but you are the one they ask for when things get difficult. You've been on a dozen exploratory missions in new systems. It's not made you rich, but it has made you one of the most influential men on Sarai. Why do *you* treat me like a human being?'

Nakamura considered it gravely. 'Well,' he decided, 'I cannot consider politics important enough to quarrel about.'

'I see.' A little embarrassed, Umfando changed the subject, 'I can get you on a military transport to Batu tomorrow, if you wish. Drop you off at the 'caster station.'

'Thank you, but I have already engaged passage on the regular intersatellite ferry.'

'Uh . . . did you ask for the *Cross* berth?'

'No. I had served a few watches on her, of course, like everyone else. A good ship. A little outmoded now, perhaps, but well and honestly made. The Guild offered me the position, and since I had no other commitments, I accepted.'

Guild offers were actually assignments for the lower

22

ranks of spacemen, Umfando knew. A man of Naka-mura's standing could have refused. But maybe the way you attained such prestige was by never refusing.

'Do you expect any trouble?' he asked.

'One is never certain. The great human mistake is to anticipate. The totally relaxed and unexpectant man is the one prepared for whatever may happen: he does not have to get out of an inappropriate posture before he can react.'

'Ha! Maybe judo ought to be required for all pilots.'

'No. I do not think the coerced mind ever really learns an art.'

Nakamura saw his house ahead. It stood on the edge of town, half screened by Terrestrial bamboo. He had spent much time on the garden which surrounded it; many visitors were kind enough to call his garden beautiful. He sighed. A gracious house, a good and faithful wife, four promising children, health and achievement . . . What more could a man reasonably ask? He told himself that his remembrances of Kyoto were hazed, he had left Earth as a very young boy. Surely this serene and uncrowded Sarai offered more than poor tortured antheap Earth gave even to her over-lords. And yet some mornings he woke up with the temple bells of Kyoto still chiming in his ears.

He stopped at the gate. 'Will you honor my home for a cup of tea?' he asked.

'No thanks,' said Umfando, almost roughly. 'You've a family to . . . to say goodbye to. I will see you when – '

Fire streaked across the sky. For an instant Il-Khan himself was lost in blue flame. The bolide struck some-where among the mountains. A sheet of pure outraged energy flared above ragged peaks. Then smoke and dust swirled up like a devil, and moments afterward thunder came banging down through the valley.

Umfando whistled. 'That was a monster!'

'A . . . yes . . . most unusual . . . yes, yes.' Nakamura stammered something, somehow he bowed good night and somehow he kept from running along the path to his roof. But as he walked, he began to shake.

It was only a meteorite, he told himself frantically. Only a meteorite. The space around a giant star, a close double, like Capella, and especially around its biggest planet, was certain to be full of cosmic junk. Billions of meteors hit Sarai every day. Hundreds of them got through to the surface. But Sarai was as big as Earth, he told himself. Sarai had oceans, deserts, uninhabited plains and forests . . . why, even on Sarai you were more likely to be killed by lightning than by a meteorite and – and –

*Oh, the jewel in the lotus!* he cried out. *I am afraid. I am afraid of the black sun.*

# 4

IT WAS raining again, but no one on Krasna pays attention to that. They wear a few light nonabsorbent garments and welcome the rain on their bodies, a moment's relief from saturated hot air. The clouds thin overhead, so that the land glimmers with watery brightness, sometimes even the uppermost clouds break apart and Tau Ceti spears a blinding reddish shaft through smoke-blue masses and silvery rain.

Chang Sverdlov rode into Dynamogorsk with a hornbeast lashed behind his saddle. It had been a dangerous chase, through the tidal marshes and up over the bleak heights of Czar Nicholas IV Range, but he needed evidence to back his story, that he had only been going out to hunt. Mukerji, the chief intelligence officer of the Protectorate garrison, was getting suspicious, God rot his brain.

Two soldiers came along the elevated sidewalk. Rain drummed on their helmets and sluiced off the slung rifles. Earth soldiers went in armed pairs on a street like Trumpet Road: for a Krasnan swamp-rancher, fisher, miner, logger, trapper, brawling away his accumulated loneliness, with a skinful of vodka or rice wine, a fluff-headed *fille-de joie* to impress, and a sullen suspicion that the dice had been loaded, was apt to unlimber his weapons when he saw a blueback.

Sverdlov contented himself with spitting at their boots, which were about level with his head. It went unnoticed in the downpour. And in the noise, and crowding, and blinking lights, with thunder above the city's gables. He clucked to his saurian and guided her toward the middle of the slough called Trumpet Road. Its excitement lifted his anger a bit. *I'll report in,* he told himself, *and go wheedle an advance from the Guild bank, and then make up six weeks of bushranging in a way the joyhouses will remember!*

He turned off on the Avenue of Tigers and stopped before a certain inn. Tethering his lizard and throwing the guard a coin, he entered the taproom. It was as full of men and racket as usual. He shouldered up to the bar. The landlord recognised him; Sverdlov was a very big and solid young man, bullet-headed, crop-haired, with a thick nose and small brown eyes in a pockmarked face. The landlord drew a mug of kvass, spiked it with vodka, and set it out. He nodded toward the ceiling. 'I will tell her you are here,' he said, and left.

Sverdlov leaned on the bar, one hand resting on a pistol butt, the other holding up his drink. *I could wish it really were one of the upstairs girls expecting me,* he thought. *Do we need all this melodrama of codes, countersigns, and cell organisation?* He considered the seething of near-naked men in the room. A chess game, a card game, a dirty joke, an Indian wrestling match, a brag, a wheedle, an incipient fight: his own Krasnans! It hardly seemed possible that any of those ears could have been hired by the Protector, and yet ...

The landlord came back. 'She's here and ready for you,' he grinned. A couple of nearby men guffawed coarsely. Sverdlov tossed off his drink, lit one of the cheap cigars he favored, and pushed through to the stairs.

At the end of a third-floor corridor he rapped on a door. A voice invited him in. The room beyond was small and drably furnished, but its window looked down a straight street to the town's end and a sudden feathery splendor of rainbow trees. Lightning flimmered through the bright rain of Krasna. Sverdlov wondered scornfully if Earth had jungle and infinite promise on any doorstep.

He closed the door and nodded at the two men who sat waiting. He knew fat Li-Tsung; the gaunt Arabic-looking fellow was strange to him, and neither asked for an introduction.

Li-Tsung raised an eyebrow. Sverdlov said, 'It is going well. They were having some new troubles – the aero-spores were playing merry hell with the electrical insulation – but I think I worked out a solution. The Wetlanders are keeping our boys amply fed, and there is no indication anyone has betrayed them. Yet.'

The thin man asked, 'This is the clandestine bomb factory?'

'No,' said Li-Tsung. 'It is time you learned of these matters, especially when you are leaving the system today. This man has been helping direct something more import-ant than small-arms manufacture. They are tooling up out there to make interplanetary missiles.'

'What for?' answered the stranger. 'Once the Fellow-ship has seized the mattercaster, it will be years before reinforcements can arrive from any other system. You'll have time enough to build heavy armament then.' He glanced inquiringly at Sverdlov. Li-Tsung nodded. 'In fact,' said the thin man, 'my division is trying to so organ-ise things that there will be no closer Protectorate forces than Earth itself. Simultaneous revolution on a dozen planets. Then it would be at least two decades before spaceships could reach Tau Ceti.'

'Ah,' grunted Sverdlov. He lowered his hairy body into a chair. His cigar jabbed at the thin man. 'Have you ever thought, the Earthlings are no fools? The mattercaster for the Tau Ceti System is up there on Moon Two. Sure. We seize it, or destroy it. But is it the *only* transceiver around?'

The thin man choked. Li-Tsung murmured, 'This is not for the rank and file. There is enough awe of Earth already, to hold the people back. But in point of fact, the Protector is an idiot if there is not at least one asteroid in some unlikely orbit, with a heavy-duty 'caster mounted on it. We can expect the Navy in our skies within hours of the independence proclamation. We must be prepared to fight!'

'But – ' said the thin man, 'but this means it will take years more to make ready than I thought. I had hoped – '

'The Centaurians rebelled prematurely, forty years ago,' said Li-Tsung. 'Let us never forget the lesson Do you want to be lobotomised?'

There was silence for a while. Rain hammered on the roof. Down in the street, a couple of rangers just in from the Uplands were organising an impromptu saurian fight.

'Well,' said Sverdlov at last. 'I'd better not stay here.'

'Oh, but you should,' said Li-Tsung. 'You are supposedly visiting a woman, do you remember?'

Sverdlov snorted impatience, but reached for the little chess set in his pouch. 'Who'll play me a quick game, then?'

'Are the bright lights that attractive?' asked Li-Tsung.

Sverdlov spoke an obscenity. 'I've spent nearly my whole leave chasing through the bush and up into the Czar,' he said. 'I'll be off to Thovo – or worse yet, to Krimchak or Cupra or the Belt, Thovo has a settlement at least – for weeks. Months perhaps! Let me relax a little first.'

'As a matter of fact,' said Li-Tsung, 'your next berth has already been assigned, and it is not to any of those places. It is outsystem.' In his public *persona*, he was a minor official in the local branch of the Astronautical Guild.

'What?' Sverdlov cursed for a steady minute. 'You mean I'm to be locked up for a month on some stinking ship in the middle of interstellar space, and – '

'Calmly, please, calmly. You won't be standing a routine single-handed just-in-case watch. This will be rather more interesting. You will be on the XA463, the *Southern Cross*.'

Sverdlov considered. He had taken his turn on the stellar vessels, but had no interest in them: they were a chore, one of the less desirable aspects of a spaceman's life. He had even been on duty when a new system was entered, but it had thrilled him not. Its planets turned out to be poisonous hells; he had finished his hitch and gone home before they even completed the transceiver station, the devil could drink his share of the dedication party.

'I don't know which of them that would be,' he said.

'It is bound for Alpha Crucis. Or was. Several years ago, the photographs taken by its instruments were routinely robo-analysed on Earth. There were discrepancies. Chiefly, some of the background stars were displaced, the Einstein effect of mass on light rays. A more careful study revealed there was a feeble source of long radio waves in that direction. They appear to be the dying gasp of a star.'

Since Sverdlov's work involved him with the atomic nucleus, he could not help arguing, 'I don't think so. The dying gasp, as you put it, would be gravitational potential energy, released as radiation when a star's own fires are all exhausted. But a thing so cold it only emits in the far radio frequencies . . . I'd say that was merely some kind of turbulence in what passes for an atmosphere. That the star isn't just dying, it's *dead*.'

'I don't know,' shrugged Li-Tsung. 'Perhaps no one does. This expedition will be to answer such questions. They gave up on Alpha Crucis for the time being and decelerated the ship toward this black star. It is arriving there now. The next personnel will take up an orbit and make the initial studies. You are the engineer.'

Sverdlov drew heavily on his cigar. 'Why me?' he protested. 'I'm an interplanetary man. Except for those damned interstellar tours, I've never even been out of the Tau Ceti System.'

'That may be one reason you were picked,' said Li-Tsung. 'The Guild does not like its men too provincial in outlook.'

'Surely,' sneered Sverdlov. 'We colonials can travel

29

anywhere we please, except to Earth. Only our goods go to Earth without special permission.'

'You need not recruit us into the Fellowship of Independence,' said the thin man in a parched voice.

Sverdlov clamped teeth together and got out through stiff lips, 'There will be Earthlings aboard, won't there? It's asking for trouble, to put me on the same ship as an Earthling.'

'You will be very polite and cooperative,' said Li-Tsung sharply. 'There are other reasons for your assignment. I cannot say much, but you can guess that we have sympathisers, even members, in the Guild . . . on a higher level than spacehand! It is possible that something of potential military value will be learned from the dark star. Who knows? Something about force fields or – Use your own imagination. It can do no harm to have a Fellowship man on the *Cross*. It may do some good. You will report to me when you return.'

'Very well, very well,' grumbled Sverdlov. 'I can stand a month or two of Earthlings, I suppose.'

'You will get your official orders soon,' Li-Tsung told him. He glanced at his watch. 'I think you can run along now; you have a reputation as a, hm-m, fast worker. Enjoy yourself.'

'And don't get talking drunk,' said the thin man.

Sverdlov paused in the doorway. 'I don't,' he said. 'I wouldn't be alive now if I did.'

# 5

THE Authority booked first-class passages for all expeditionary personnel, which in the case of a hop up to the Moon meant a direct ferry traveling at one gee all the way. Standing by the observation window, an untasted drink in his hand, David Ryerson remarked, 'You know, this is only the third time I've ever been off Earth. And the other two, we transshipped at Satellite and went free-fall most of the way.'

'Sounds like fun,' said Maclaren. 'I must try it sometime.'

'You . . . in your line of work . . . you must go to the Moon quite often,' said Ryerson shyly.

Maclaren nodded. 'Mount Ambarzumian Observatory, on Farside. Still a little dust and gas to bother us, of course, but I'll let the purists go out to Pluto Satellite and bring me back their plates.'

'And . . . No. Forgive me.' Ryerson shook his blond head.

'Go on.' Maclaren, seated in a voluptuous formfit lounger, offered a box of cigarets. He thought he knew Ryerson's type, serious, gifted, ambitious, but awe-smitten at the gimcrack fact of someone's hereditary technic rank. 'Go ahead,' he invited. 'I don't embarrass easy.'

'I was only wondering . . . who paid for all your trips . . . the observatory or –'

'Great ancestors! The observatory!' Maclaren threw back his head and laughed with the heartiness of a man who had never had to be very cautious. It rang above the

31

low music and cultivated chatter; even the ecdysiast paused an instant on her stage.

'My dear old colleague,' said Maclaren, 'I not only pay my own freight, I am expected to contribute generously toward the expenses of the institution. At least,' he added, 'my father is. But where else would money for pure research come from? You can't tax it out of the lower commons, y'know. They haven't got it. The upper commons are already taxed to the limit, short of pushing them back down into the hand-to-mouth masses. And the Protectorate rests on a technic class serving but not paying. That's the theory, anyhow: in practice, of course, a lot of 'em do neither. But how else would you support abstract science, except by patronage? Thank the Powers for the human snob instinct, it keeps both research and art alive.'

Ryerson looked alarmed, glanced about as if expecting momentary arrest, finally lowered himself to the edge of a chair and almost whispered, 'Yes, sir, yes, I know, naturally. I was just not so . . . so familiar with the details of . . . financing.'

'Eh? But how could you have missed learning? You trained to be a scientist, didn't you?'

Ryerson stared out at Earth, sprawling splendor across the constellations. 'I set out to be a spaceman,' he said, blushing. 'But in the last couple of years I got more interested in gravitics, had to concentrate too much on catching up in that field to . . . well . . . also, I was planning to emigrate, so I wasn't interested in –The colonies need trained men. The opportunities – '

*Pioneering is an unlimited chance to become the biggest frog, provided the puddle is small enough,* thought Maclaren. But he asked aloud, politely, 'Where to?'

'Rama. The third planet of Washington 5584.'

'Hm? Oh, yes. The new one, the G0 dwarf. Uh, how far from here?'

'Ninety-seven light years. Rama has just passed the five-year survey test.' Ryerson leaned forward, losing

32

shyness in his enthusiasm. 'Actually, sir, Rama is the most nearly terrestroid planet they have yet found. The biochemistry is so similar to Earth's that one can even eat some of the native plants. Oh, and there are climatic zones, oceans, forests, mountains, a single big moon – '

'And thirty years of isolation,' said Maclaren. 'Nothing connecting you to the universe but a voice.'

Ryerson reddened again. 'Does that matter so much?' he asked aggressively. 'Are we losing a great deal by that?'

'I suppose not,' said Maclaren. *Your lives, perhaps,* he thought. *Remember the Shadow Plague on New Kashmir? Or your children – there was the mutation virus on Gondwana. Five years is not long enough to learn a planet; the thirty-year quarantine is an arbitrary minimum. And, of course, there are the more obvious and spectacular things, which merely kill colonists without threatening the human race. Storms, quakes, morasses, volcanoes, meteorites. Cumulative poisoning. Wild animals. Unsuspected half-intelligent aborigines. Strangeness, loneliness, madness. It's no wonder the colonies which survive develop their own cultures. It's no wonder they come to think of Earth as a parasite on their own tedious heroisms. Of course, with ten billion people, and a great deal of once arable country sterilised by radiation, Earth has little choice.*

*What I would like to know is, why does anyone emigrate in the first place? The lessons are ghastly enough; why do otherwise sensible people, like this boy, refuse to learn them?*

'Oh, well,' he said aloud. He signaled the waiter. 'Refuel us, chop-chop.'

Ryerson looked in some awe at the chit which the other man thumbprinted. He could not suppress it, 'Do you always travel first class to the Moon?'

Maclaren put a fresh cigaret between his lips and touched his lighter-ring to the end. His smile cocked it at a wry angle. 'I suppose,' he answered, 'I have always traveled first class through life.'

The ferry made turnover with spilling a drink or a passenger and back down on to Tycho Port. Maclaren adjusted without a thought to Lunar gravity, Ryerson turned a little green and swallowed a pill. But even in his momentary distress, Ryerson was bewildered at merely walking through a tube to a monorail station. Third-class passengers must submit to interminable official bullying: safety regulations, queues, assignment to hostel. Now, within minutes, he was again on soft cushions, staring through crystalline panes at the saw-toothed magnificence of mountains.

When the train got under way, he gripped his hands together, irrationally afraid. It took him a while to hunt down the reason: the ghost of his father's God, ranting at pride and sloth from the tomb which the son had erected.

'Let's eat,' said Maclaren. 'I chose this train with malice aforethought. It's slow enough so we man enjoy our meal enroute, and the chef puts his heart into the oysters won-ton.'

'I'm not . . . not hungry,' stammered Ryerson.

Maclaren's dark, hooked face flashed a grin. 'That's what cocktails and hors d'oeuvres are for, lad. Stuff yourself. If it's true what I've heard of deep-space rations, we're in for a dreary month or two.'

'You mean you've never been on an interstellar ship?'

'Of course not. Never been beyond the Moon in my life. Why should I do any such ridiculous thing?'

Maclaren's cloak swirled like fire as he led the way toward the diner. Beneath an iridescent white tunic, his legs showed muscular and hairless, down to the tooled-leather buskins; the slant of the beret on his head was pure insolence. Ryerson, trailing drably behind in space-man's gray coveralls, felt bitterness. *What the hell have I been dragged away from Tamara for? Does this peacock know a mass from a scroll in the ground? He's hired himself a toy, is all, because for a while he's bored with wine and women . . . and Tamara is locked away on a rock with a self-righteous old beast who hates the sound of her name!*

As they sat down at their table, Maclaren went on, 'But this is too good a chance to pass up. I found me a tame mathematician last year and sicced him on to the Schrödinger equation – Sugimoto's relativistic version, I mean; Yuen postulates too bloody much for my taste – anyhow, he worked it out for the quantities involved in a dark star, mass and gravitational intensities and cetera. His results make us both wonder if such a body doesn't go over to an entirely new stage of degeneracy at the core. One gigantic neutron? Well, maybe that's too fantastic. But consider – '

And while the monorail ran on toward Farside, Maclaren left the Interhuman language quite behind him. Ryerson could follow tensors, even when scribbled on a menu, but Maclaren had some new function, symbolised by a pneumatic female outline, that *reduced* to a generalised tensor under certain conditions. Ryerson stepped out on Farside, two hours later, with his brain rotating.

He had heard of the cyclopean installations which fill the whole of Yukawa Crater and spread out on to the plains beyond. Who has not? But all he saw on his first visit was a gigantic concourse, a long slideway tunnel, and a good many uniformed technicians. He made some third mention of his disappointment to Maclaren. The New Zealander nodded: 'Exactly. There's more romance, more sense of distance covered, and a devil of a lot better scenery in an afternoon on the bay, than in a fifty-light-year leap. I say space travel is overrated. And it's a fact, I've heard, that spacemen themselves prefer the interplanetary runs. They take the dull interstellar watches as a matter of duty, by turns.'

Here and there the tunnel branched off, signs indicating the way to Alpha Centauri Jump, Tau Ceti Jump, Epsilon Eridani Jump, all the long-colonised systems. Those were for passengers; freight went by other beams. There was no great bustle along any of the tubes. Comparatively few

35

Earthlings had occasion to visit outsystem on business, still fewer could afford it for pleasure, and of course no colonial came here without a grudging okay. The Protector had trouble enough; he was not going to expose the mother planet and its restless billions to new ideas born under new skies, nor let any more colonials than he could help see first-hand what an inferior position they held. That was the real reason for the ban, every educated Terrestrial knew as much. The masses, being illiterate, swallowed a vague official excuse about trade policy.

The branches leading to Sirius Jump, Procyon Jump, and the other attained but uncolonisable systems, were almost deserted. Little came from such places – perhaps an occasional gem or exotic chemical. But relay stations had been established there, for 'casting to more useful planets.

Ryerson's heart leaped when he passed a newly activated sign: an arrow and WASHINGTON 5584 JUMP burning above. *That* tunnel would be filled, come next week!

He should have been in the line. And Tamara. Well, there would be later waves. His passage was already paid for, he had no difficulty about transferring to another section.

To make conversation, he said through a tightness, 'Where are the bulkheads?'

'Which ones?' asked Maclaren absently.

'Safety bulkheads. A receiver does fail once in a great while, you know. That's why the installations here are spread out so much, why every star has a separate 'caster. There's a vast amount of energy involved in each transmission – one reason why a 'casting is more expensive than transportation by spaceship. Even a small increment, undissipated, can melt a whole chamber.'

'Oh, yes. That.' Maclaren had let Ryerson get pompous about the obvious because it was plain he needed something to bolster himself. What itched the kid, any-how? One should think that when the Authority offered a fledgling a post on an expedition as fundamental as this – Of course, it had upset Ryerson's plans of emigration. But not importantly. There was no danger he would find all the choice sites on Rama occupied if he came several weeks late: too few people had the fare as it was.

Maclaren said, 'I see what you mean. Yes, the bulk-heads are there, but recessed into the walls and camou-flaged. You don't want to emphasise possible danger to the cash customers, eh? Some technic might get annoyed and make trouble.'

'Some day,' said Ryerson, 'they'll reduce the energy margin needed; and they'll figure how to reproduce a Frank tube, rather than manufacture it. Record the pattern and recreate from a matter bank. Then anyone can afford to ride the beams. Interplanetary ships, even air and surface craft, will become obsolete.'

Maclaren made no answer. He had sometimes thought, more or less idly, about the unrealised potentialities of mattercasting. Hard to say whether personal immortality would be a good thing or not. Not for the masses, surely! Too many of them as it was. But a select few, like Terangi Maclaren – or was it worth the trouble? Even given boats, chess, music, the Nō Drama, beautiful women and beautiful spectroscopes, life could get heavy.

As for matter transmission, the difficulty and hence the expense lay in the complexity of the signal. Consider an adult human. There are some $10^{14}$ cells in him, each an elaborate structure involving many proteins with molecular weights in the millions. You had to scan every one of those molecules – identify it structurally, ticket its momentary energy levels, and place it in proper spatio-temporal relationship to every other molecule – as nearly simultaneously as the laws of physics permitted. You couldn't take a man apart, or reassemble him, in more than a few microseconds; he wouldn't survive it. You

37

couldn't even transmit a recognisable beefsteak in much less of a hurry.

So the scanning beam went through and through, like a blade of energy. It touched every atom in its path, was modified thereby, and flashed that modification on to the transmitter matrix. But such fury destroyed. The scanned object was reduced to gas, so quickly that only an oscilloscope could watch the process. The gas was sucked into the destructor chamber and atomically condensed in the matter bank; in time it would become an incoming passenger, or incoming freight. In a sense, the man had died.

If you could record the signal which entered the transmitter matrix, you could keep such a record indefinitely, recreate the man and his instantaneous memories, thoughts, habits, prejudices, hopes and loves and hates and horrors, a thousand years afterward. You could create a billion identical men. Or, more practically, a single handmade prototype could become a billion indistinguishable copies; nothing would be worth more than any handful of dirt. Or ... superimpose the neurone trace-patterns, memories, of a lifetime, on to a recorded twenty-year-old body, be born again and live forever!

The signal was too complex, though. An unpromising research program went on. Perhaps in a few centuries they would find some trick which would enable them to record a man, or even a Frank tube. Meanwhile, transmission had to be simultaneous with scanning. The signal went out. Probably it would be relayed a few times. Eventually the desired receiving chamber got it. The receiver matrix, powered by dying atomic nuclei, flung gases together, formed higher elements, formed molecules and cells and dreams according to the signal, in microseconds. It was designed as an energy-consuming process, for obvious reasons: packing fraction energy was dissipated in gravitic and magnetic fields, to help shape the man (or the beefsteak, or the spaceship, or the colonial planet's produce). He left the receiving chamber and went about his business.

*A mono-isotopic element is a simple enough signal to record,* Maclaren reminded himself, *though even that requires a houseful of transistor elements. So this civilisation can afford to be extravagant with metals – can use pure mercury as the raw material of a spaceship's blast, for instance. But we still eat our bread in the sweat of some commoner's brow.*

Not for the first time, but with no great indignation – life was too short for anything but amusement at the human race – Maclaren wondered if the recording problem really was as difficult as the physicists claimed. No government likes revolutions, and molecular duplication would revolutionise society beyond imagining. Just think how they had to guard the stations as it was, and stick them out here on the Moon . . . otherwise, even today, some fanatic could steal a tube of radium from a hospital and duplicate enough to sterilise a planet!

'Oh, well,' he said, half aloud.

They reached the special exploratory section and entered an office. There was red tape to unsnarl. Ryerson let Maclaren handle it, and spent the time trying to understand that soon the pattern which was himself would be embodied in new shaped atoms, a hundred light-years from Tamara. It wouldn't penetrate. It was only words.

Finally the papers were stamped. The transceivers to/from an interstellar spaceship could handle several hundred kilos at a time; Maclaren and Ryerson went together. They had a moment's wait because of locked safety switches on the *Southern Cross*: someone else was arriving or departing ahead of them.

'Watch that first step,' said Maclaren. 'It's a honey.'

'What?' Ryerson blinked at him, uncomprehending.

The circuit closed. There was no sensation, the process went too fast.

The scanner put its signal into the matrix. The matrix modulated the carrier wave. But such terminology is mere slang, borrowed from electronics. You cannot have a 'wave' when you have no velocity, and gravitational

39

forces do not. (This is a more accurate rendition of the common statement that 'gravitation propagates at an infinite speed'.) Inconceivable energies surged within a thermonuclear fire chamber; nothing controlled them, nothing could control them, but the force fields they themselves generated. Matter pulsed in and out of existence *qua* matter, from particle to gamma ray quantum and back. Since quanta have no rest mass, the pulsations disturbed the geometry of space according to the laws of Einsteinian mechanics. Not much: gravitation is feebler than magnetism or electricity. Were it not for the resonance effect, the signal would have been smothered in 'noise' a few kilometers away. Even as it was, there were many relayings across the parsecs, until the matrix on the *Cross* reacted. And yet in one sense no time at all had passed; and no self-respecting mathematician would have called the 'beam' by such a name. It was, however, a signal, the only signal which relativity physics allowed to go faster than light – and, after all, it did not really *go*, it simply *was*.

Despite the pill inside him, Ryerson felt as if the bottom had dropped out of the world. He grabbed for a handhold. The after-image of the transmitter chamber yielded to the coils and banks of the receiver room on a spaceship. He hung weightless, a thousand billion billion kilometers from Earth.

# 6

FORWARD of the 'casting chambers, 'above' them during acceleration, were fuel deck, gyros, and air-renewal plant. Then you passed through the observation deck, where instruments and laboratory equipment crowded together. A flimsy wall around the shaftway marked off the living quarters: folding bunks, galley, bath, table, benches, shelves, lockers, all crammed into a six-meter circle.

Seiichi Nakamura wrapped one leg casually around a stanchion, to keep himself from drifting in air currents, and made a ceremony out of leafing through the log book in his hands. It gave the others a chance to calm down, and the yellow-haired boy, David Ryerson, seemed to need it. The astrophysicist, Maclaren, achieved the unusual feat of lounging in free fall; he puffed an expensive Earthside cigaret and wrinkled his patrician nose at the pervading smell of an old ship, two hundred years of cooking and sweat and machine oil. The big, ugly young engineer, Sverdlov, merely looked sullen. Nakamura had never met any of them before.

'Well, gentlemen,' he said at last. 'Pardon me, I had to check the data recorded by the last pilot. Now I know approximately where we are at.' He laughed with polite self-deprecation. 'Of course you are all familiar with the articles. The pilot is captain. His duty is to guide the ship where the chief scientist – Dr. Maclaren-san in this case – wishes, within the limits of safety as determined by his own judgment. In case of my death or disability, command devolves upon the engineer, ah, Sverdlov-san, and you are to return home as soon as practicable.

Yes-s-s. But I am sure we will all have a most pleasant and instructive expedition together.'

He felt the banality of his words. It was the law, and a wise one, that authority be defined at once if there were non-Guild personnel aboard. Some pilots contented themselves with reading the regulations aloud, but it had always seemed an unnecessarily cold procedure to Nakamura. Only . . . he saw a sick bewilderment in Ryerson's eyes, supercilious humor in Maclaren's, angry impatience in Sverdlov's . . . his attempt at friendliness had gone flat.

'We do not operate so formally,' he went on in a lame fashion. 'We shall post a schedule of housekeeping duties and help each other, yes? Well. That is for later. Now as to the star, we have some approximate data and estimates taken by previous watches. It appears to have about four times the mass of Sol; its radius is hardly more than twice Earth's, possibly less; it emits detectably only in the lower radio frequencies, and even that is feeble. I have a quick reading of the spectrum which may interest you, Dr. Maclaren.'

The big dark man reached out for it. His brows went up. 'Now this,' he said, 'is the weirdest collection of wavelengths I ever saw.' He flickered experienced eyes along the column of numbers. 'Seems to be a lot of triplets, but the lines appear so broad, judging from the probable errors given, that I can't be sure without more careful – hm-m.' Glancing back at Nakamura, 'Just where are we with relation to the star?'

'Approximately two million kilometers from the center of its mass. We are being drawn toward it, of course, since an orbit has not yet been established, but have enough radial velocity of our own to – '

'Never mind.' The sophistication dropped from Maclaren like a tunic. He said with a boy's eagerness, 'I would like to get as near the star as possible. How close do you think you can put us?'

Nakamura smiled. He had a feeling Maclaren could

prove likeable. 'Too close isn't prudent. There would be meteors.'

'Not around this one!' exclaimed Maclaren. 'If physical theory is anything but mescaline dreams, a dead star is the clinker of a supernova. Any matter orbiting in its neighborhood became incandescent gas long ago.'

'Atmosphere?' asked Nakamura dubiously. 'Since we have nothing to see by, except starlight, we could hit its air.'

'Hm. Yes. I suppose it would have some. But not very deep: too compressed to be deep. In fact, the radio photosphere, from which the previous watches estimated the star's diameter, must be nearly identical with the fringes of atmosphere.'

'It would also take a great deal of reaction mass to pull us back out of its attraction, if we got too close,' said Nakamura. He unclipped the specialised slide rule at his belt and made a few quick computations. 'In fact, this vessel cannot escape from a distance much less than three-quarters million kilometers, if there is to be reasonable amount of mass left for maneuvering around afterward. And I am sure you wish to explore regions farther from the star, yes-s-s? However, I am willing to go that close.'

Maclaren smiled. 'Good enough. How long to arrive?'

'I estimate three hours, including time to establish the orbit.' Nakamura looked around at their faces. 'If everyone is prepared to go on duty, it is best we get into the desired path at once.'

'Not even a cup of tea first?' grumbled Sverdlov.

Nakamura nodded at Maclaren and Ryerson. 'You gentlemen will please prepare tea and sandwiches, and take them to the engineer and myself in about ninety minutes.'

'Now, wait!' protested Maclaren. 'We've hardly arrived. I haven't even looked at my instruments. I have to set up –'

'In ninety minutes, if you will be so kind. Very well,

43

let us assume our posts.'

Nakamura turned from Maclaren's suddenly mutinous look and Sverdlov's broad grin. He entered the shaftway and pulled himself along it by the rungs. Through the transparent plastic he saw the observation deck fall behind. The boat deck was next, heavy storage levels followed, and then he was forward, into the main turret.

It was a clear plastic bubble, unshuttered now when the sole outside illumination was a wintry blaze of stars. Floating toward the controls, Nakamura grew aware of the silence. So quiet. So uncountably many stars. The constellations were noticeably distorted, some altogether foreign. He searched a crystal darkness for Capella, but the bulge of the ship hid it from him. No use looking for Sol without a telescope, here on the lonely edge of the known.

Fear or raw emptiness lay tightly coiled within him. He smothered it by routine: strapped himself before the console, checked the instruments one by one, spoke with Sverdlov down the length of the ship. His fingers chattered out a computation on a set of keys, he fed the tape to the robot, he felt a faint tug as the gyros woke up, swiveling the vessel into position for blast. Even now, at the end of acceleration to half light-speed and deceleration to a few hundred kilometers per second, the *Cross* bore several tons of reaction-mass mercury. The total mass, including hull, equipment, and payload, was a bit over one kiloton. Accordingly, her massive gyroscopes needed half an hour to turn her completely around.

Waiting, he studied the viewscreens. Since he must back down on his goal, what they showed him was more important than what his eyes saw through this turret in the nose. He could not make out the black sun. *Well, what do you expect?* he asked himself angrily. *It must be occulting a few stars, but there are too many.* 'Dr. Maclaren,' he said into the intercom, 'can you give me a radio directional on the target, as a check?'

'Aye, aye.' A surly answer. Maclaren resented having to put his toys to work. He would rather have been taking spectra, reading ionoscopes, gulping gas and dust samples from outside into his analysers, every centimeter of the way. Well, he would just have to get those data when they receded from the star again.

Nakamura's eyes strayed down the ship herself, as shown in the viewscreens. *Old,* he thought. *The very nation which built her has ceased to exist. But good work. A man's work outlives his hands. Though what remains of the little ivory figures my father carved to ornament our house? What chance did my brother have to create, before he shriveled in my arms? No!* He shut off the thought, like a surgeon clamping a vein, and refreshed his memory of the *Cygnus* class.

This hull was a sphere of reinforced self-sealing plastic, fifty meters across, its outside smoothness broken by hatches, ports, airlocks, and the like. The various decks sliced it in parallel planes. After, diametrically opposite this turret, the hull opened on the fire chamber. And thence ran two thin metal skeletons, thirty meters apart, a hundred meters long, like radio masts or ancient oil derricks. They comprised two series of rings, a couple of centimeters in diameter, with auxiliary wiring and a spidery framework holding it all together – the ion accelerators, built into and supported by the gravitic transceiver web.

'A ten-second test blast, if you please, Engineer Sverdlov,' said Nakamura.

The instruments showed him a certain unbalance in the distribution of mass within the hull. Yussuf bin Suleiman, who had just finished watch aboard the ship and gone back to Earth, was sloppy about . . . no, it was unjust to think so . . . say that he had his own style of piloting. Nakamura set the pumps to work. Mercury ran from the fuel deck to the trim tanks.

By then the ship was pointed correctly and it was time to start decelerating again. 'Stand by for blast . . . Report

45

. . . I shall want one-point-five-seven standard gees for – "

Nakamura reeled it off almost automatically.

It rumbled in the ship. Weight came, like a sudden fist in the belly. Nakamura held his body relaxed in harness, only his eyes moved, now and then a finger touched a control. The secret of judo, of life, was to hold every part of the organism at ease except those precise tissues needed for the moment's task. Why was it so damnably difficult to put into practice?

Mercury fed through pipes and pumps, past Sverdlov's control board, past the radiation wall, into the expansion chamber and through the ioniser and so as a spray past the sunlike heart of a thermonuclear plasma. Briefly, each atom endured a rage of mesons. It broke down, gave up its mass as pure energy, which at once became proton-antiproton pairs. Magnetic fields separated them as they were born: positive and negative particles fled down the linear accelerators. The plasma, converting the death of matter directly to electricity, charged each ring at a successively higher potential. When the particles emerged from the last ring, they were traveling at three-fourths the speed of light.

At such an exhaust velocity, no great mass had to be discharged. Nor was the twin stream visible; it was too efficient. Sensitive instruments might have detected a pale gamma-colored splotch, very far behind the ship, as a few opposite charges finally converged on each other, but that effect was of no importance.

The process was energy-eating. It had to be. Otherwise surplus heat would have vaporised the ship. The plasma furnished energy to spare. The process was a good deal more complex than a few words can describe, and yet less so than an engineer accustomed to more primitive branches of his art might imagine.

Nakamura gave himself up to the instruments. Their readings checked out with his running computation. The *Cross* was approaching the black star in a complex spiral curve, the resultant of several velocities and two accelerating vectors, which would become a nearly circular orbit 750,000 kilometers out.

He started to awareness of time when young Ryerson came up the shaftway rungs. 'Oh,' he exclaimed.

'Tea, sir,' said the boy shyly.

'Thank you. Ah . . . set it down there, please . . . the regulations forbid entering this turret during blast without inquiring of the – No, no. Please!' Nakamura waved a hand, laughing. 'You did not know. There is no harm done.'

He saw Ryerson, stopped under one and a half gravities, lift a heavy head to the foreign stars. The Milky Way formed a cold halo about his tangled hair. Nakamura asked gently, 'This is your first time in extrasolar space, yes?'

'Y-yes, sir.' Ryerson licked his lips. The blue eyes were somehow hazy, unable to focus closer than the nebulae.

'Do not – ' Nakamura paused. He had been about to say, 'Do not be afraid,' but it might hurt. He felt after words. 'Space is a good place to meditate,' he said. 'I use the wrong word, of course. "Meditation," in Zen, consists more of an attempt at identification with the universe than verbalised thinking. What I mean to say,' he floundered, 'is this. Some people feel themselves so helplessly small out here that they become frightened. Others, remembering that home is no more than a step away through the transmitter, become careless and arrogant, the cosmos merely a set of meaningless numbers to them. Both attitudes are wrong, and have killed men. But if you think of yourself as being a *part* of everything else – integral – the same forces in you which shaped the suns – do you see?'

' "The heavens declare the glory of God," ' whispered Ryerson, ' "and the firmament showeth His handiwork". . . . It is a terrible thing to fall into the hands of the living God.'

He had not been listening, and Nakamura did not

47

understand English. The pilot sighed, 'I think you had best return to the observation deck,' he said. 'Dr. Maclaren may have need of you.'

Ryerson nodded mutely and went back down the shaft.

*I preach a good theory,* Nakamura told himself. *Why can I not practice it? Because a stone fell from heaven on to Sarai, and suddenly father and mother and sister and house were not. Because Hideki died in my arms, after the universe had casually tortured him. Because I shall never see Kyoto again, where every morning was full of cool bells. Because I am a slave of myself.*

*And yet,* he thought, *sometimes I have achieved peace. And only in space.*

Now he saw the dead sun through a viewscreen, when his ship swung so that it transitted the Milky Way. It was a tiny blackness. The next time around, it had grown. He wondered if it was indeed blacker than the sky. Nonsense. It should reflect starlight, should it not? But what color was metallic hydrogen? What gases overlay the metal? Space, especially here, was not absolutely black: there was a certain thin but measurable nebular cloud around the star. So conceivably the star might be blacker than the sky.

'I must ask Maclaren,' he murmured to himself. 'He can measure it, very simply, and tell me. Meditation upon the concept of blacker than total blackness is not helpful, it seems.' That brought him a wry humor, which untensed his muscles. He grew aware of weariness. It should not have been; he had only been sitting here and pressing controls. He poured a cup of scalding tea and drank noisily and gratefully.

Down and down. Nakamura fell into an almost detached state. Now the star was close, not much smaller than the Moon seen from Earth. It grew rapidly, and crawled still more rapidly around the circle of the viewscreens. Now is was as big as Batu, at closest approach to Sarai. Now it was bigger. The rhythms entered Nakamura's blood. Dimly, he felt himself become one with the ship, the fields, the immense interplay of forces. And this was why he went again and yet again into space. He touched the manual controls, assisting the robots, correcting, revising, in a pattern of unformulated but bodily known harmonies, a dance, a dream, yielding, controlling, unselfness, Nirvana, pace and wholeness. . . .

Fire!

The shock rammed Nakamura's spine against his skull. He felt his teeth clashed together. Blood from a bitten tongue welled in his mouth. Thunder roared between the walls.

He stared into the screens, clawing for comprehension. The ship was a million or so kilometers out. The black star was not quite one degree wide, snipped out of an unnamed alien constellation. The far end of the ion accelerator system was white hot. Even as Nakamura watched, the framework curled up, writhed like fingers in agony, and vaporised.

*'What's going on?'* Horror bawled from the engine room.

The thrust fell off and weight dropped sickeningly. Nakamura saw hell eat along the accelerators. He jerked his eyes around to the primary megammeter. Its needle sank down a tale of numbers. The four outermost rings were already destroyed. Even as he watched, the next one shriveled.

It could not be felt, but he knew how the star's vast hand clamped on the ship and reeled her inward.

Metal whiffed into space. Underloaded, the nuclear system howled its anger. Echoes banged between shivering decks.

'Cut!' cried Nakamura. His hand slapped the pilot's master switch.

The silence that fell, and the no-weight, were like death.

Someone's voice gabbled from the observation deck. Automatically, Nakamura chopped that interference out of the intercom circuit.

'Engineer Sverdlov,' he called. 'What happened? Do you know what is wrong?'

'No. No.' A groan. But at least the man lived. 'Somehow the – the ion streams . . . seem to have . . . gotten diverted. The focusing fields went awry. The blast struck the rings – but it couldn't happen!'

Nakamura hung on to his harness with all ten fingers. *I will not scream*, he shouted. *I will not scream.*

'The 'caster web seems to be gone too,' said a rusty machine using his throat. His brother's dead face swam among the stars, just outside the turret, and mouthed at him.

'Aye.' Sverdlov must be hunched over his own viewscreens. After a while that tingled, he said harshly, 'Not yet beyond repair. All ships carry a few replacement parts, in case of meteors or – We can repair the web and transmit ourselves out of here.'

'How long to do that job? Quickly!'

'How should I know?' A dragon snarl. Then, 'I'd have to go out and take a closer look. The damaged sections will have to be cut away. It'll probably be necessary to machine some fittings. With luck, we can do it in several hours.'

Nakamura paused. He worked his hands together, strength opposing strength; he drew slow breaths, rolled his head to loosen the neck muscles, finally closed his eyes and contemplated peace for as long as needful. And a measure of peace came. The death of this little ego was not so terrible after all, provided said ego refrained from wishing to hold Baby-san in its arms just one more time.

Almost absently, he punched the keys of the general computer. It was no surprise to see his guess verified.

'Are you there?' called Sverdlov, as if across centuries. 'Are you there, pilot?'

'Yes. I beg your pardon. Several hours to repair the web, did you say. By that time, drifting free, we will have crashed on the star.'

'What? But we're *in* orbit! Eccentric, maybe, but – '

'It is too narrow. We still have too much inward radial velocity. If the star were a single point, we would be in no danger; but it has volume. As nearly as I can determine – though there are so many uncertainties – our present orbit intersects the star. I think I can put us into a safe path before the what-ever-it-is force has quite destroyed the accelerators. Yes.'

'But you'll burn them up! And the web! We'll damage the web beyond repair!'

'Perhaps something can be improvised, once we are in orbit. But if we continue simply falling, we are dead men.'

'No!' Almost, Sverdlov shrieked. 'Listen, maybe we can repair the web in time. Maybe we'll only need a couple of hours for the job. There's a chance. But caught in an orbit, with the web melted or vaporised . . . do you know how to build one from raw metal? I don't!'

'We have a gravitics specialist aboard. If anyone can fashion us a new transmitter, he can.'

'And if he can't, we're trapped out here! To starve! Better to crash and be done!'

Nakamura's hands began to dance over the keyboard. He demanded data of the instruments, calculations of the computers, and nothing of the auto-pilot. For no machine could help steer a vessel whose thrust-engine was being unpredictably devoured. This would be a manual task.

'I am the captain,' he said, as mildly as possible.

'Not any more!'

Nakamura slapped his master switch. 'You have just been cut out of the control circuits,' he said. 'Please remain at your post.' He opened the intercom to the observation deck. 'Will the two honorable scientists be so kind as to stop the engineer from interfering with the pilot?'

# 7

FOR a moment, the rage in Chang Sverdlov was such that blackness flapped before his eyes.

When he regained himself, he found the viewscreens still painted with ruin. Starlight lay wan along the frail network of the transceiver web and the two sets of rings which it held together. At the far end the metal glowed red. A few globs of spattered stuff orbited like lunatic fireflies. Beyond the twisted burned-off end of the system, light-years dropped away to the cold blue glitter of a thousand crowding stars. The dead sun was just discernible, a flattened darkness. It seemed to be swelling visibly. Whether that was a real effect or not, Sverdlov felt the dread of falling, the no-weight horrors, like a lump in his belly.

He hadn't been afraid of null-gee since he was a child. In his cadet days, he had invented more pranks involving free fall than any two other boys. But he had never been cut off from home in this fashion. Krasna had never been more than an interplanetary flight or an interstellar Jump away.

And that cookbook pilot would starve out here to save his worthless ship?

Sverdlov unbuckled his harness. He kicked himself across the little control room, twisted among the pipes and wheels and dials of the fuel-feed section like a swimming fish, and came to the tool rack. He chose a long wrench and arrowed for the shaftway. His fury had chilled into resolution: *I don't want to kill him, but he'll have to be made to see reason. And quickly, or we really will crash!*

He was rounding the transmitter chamber when deceleration resumed. He had been going up by the usual process, grab a rung ahead of you and whip your weightless body beyond. Suddenly two Terrestrial gravities snatched him.

He closed fingers about one of the bars. His left arm straightened, with a hundred and ninety kilos behind. The hand tore loose. He let go the wrench and caught with his right arm, jamming it between a rung and the shaft wall. The impact smashed across his biceps. Then his left hand clawed fast and he hung. He heard the wrench skid past the gyro housing, hit a straight drop-off, and clang on the after radiation shield.

Gasping, he found a lower rung with his feet and sagged for a minute. The right arm was numb, until the pain woke in it. He flexed the fingers. Nothing broken.

But he was supposed to be in harness. Nakamura's calculations might demand spurts of ten or fifteen gravities, if the accelerators could still put out that much. The fear of being smeared across a bulkhead jolted into Sverdlov. He scrambled over the rungs. It was nightmarishly like climbing through glue. After a thousand years he burst into the living quarters.

Maclaren sat up in one of the bunks. 'No further, please,' he said.

The deceleration climbed a notch. His weight was iron on Sverdlov's shoulders. He started back into the shaft. 'No!' cried Ryerson. But it was Maclaren who flung off bunk harness and climbed to the deck. The brown face gleamed wet, but Maclaren smiled and said, 'Didn't you hear me?'

Sverdlov grunted and re-entered the shaft, both feet on a rung. *I can make it up to the bubble and get my hands on Nakamura's throat.* Maclaren stood for a gauging instant, as Sverdlov's foot crept toward the next rung. Finally the physicist added with a sneer in the tone,

53

'When a technic says sit, you squat . . . colonial.'

Sverdlov halted. 'What was that?' he asked slowly.

'I can haul you out of there if I must, you backwoods pig,' said Maclaren, 'but I'd rather you came to me.'

Sverdlov wondered, with an odd quick sadness, why he responded. Did an Earthling's yap make so much difference? He decided that Maclaren would probably make good on that promise to follow him up the shaft, and under this weight a fight on the rungs could kill them both. Therefore – Sverdlov's brain seemed as heavy as his bones. He climbed back and stood slumping on the observation deck. 'Well?' he said.

Maclaren folded his arms. 'Better get into a bunk,' he advised.

Sverdlov lumbered toward him. In a shimmery wisp of tunic, the Earthling looked muscular enough, but he probably massed ten kilos less, and lacked several centimeters of the Krasnan's height and reach. A few swift blows would disable him, and it might still not be too late to stop Nakamura.

'Put up your fists,' said Sverdlov hoarsely.

Maclaren unfolded his arms. A sleepy smile crossed his face. Sverdlov came in, swinging at the eagle beak. Maclaren's head moved aside. His hands came up, took Sverdlov's arm, and applied a cruel leverage. Sverdlov gasped, broke free by sheer strength, and threw a blow to the ribs. Maclaren stopped that fist with an edge-on chop at the wrist behind it; almost, Sverdlov thought he felt the bones crack. They stood toe to toe. Sverdlov drew back the other fist. Maclaren punched him in the groin. The Krasnan doubled over in a jag of anguish. Maclaren rabbit-punched him. Sverdlov went to one knee, Maclaren kicked him in the solar plexus. Sverdlov fell over and struck the floor with three gravities to help.

Through a wobbling, ringing darkness, he heard the Earthling, 'Help me with this beef, Dave.' And he felt himself dragged across the floor, somehow manhandled into a bunk and harnessed.

His mind returned. Pain stabbed and flickered through him. He struggled to sit up. 'That was an Earthman way to fight,' he pushed out through a swelling mouth.

'I don't enjoy fighting,' said Maclaren from his own bunk, 'so I got it over with as soon as possible.'

'You – ' The Krasnan lifted grotesquely heavy hands and fumbled with his harness. 'I'm going to the control turret. If you try to stop me this time –'

'You're already too late, brother Sverdlov,' said Maclaren coolly. 'Whatever you were setting out to forestall has gone irrevocably far toward happening.'

The words were a physical blow.

'It's . . . yes,' said the engineer. 'I'm too late.' The shout burst from him, 'We're all too late, now!'

'Ease back,' said Maclaren. 'Frankly, your behavior doesn't give me much confidence in your judgment about anything.'

It rumbled through the ship. That shouldn't be, thought Sverdlov's training; even full blast ought to be nearly noiseless, and this was only fractional. Sweat prickled his skin. For the first time in a violent life, he totally realised that he could die.

'I'm sorry for what I called you,' said Maclaren. 'I had to stop you, but now I apologise.'

Sverdlov made no answer. He stared up at a blank ceiling. Oddly, his first emotion, as rage ebbed, was an overwhelming sorrow. Now he would never see Krasna made free.

# 8

SILENCE and no-weight were dreamlike. For a reason obscure to himself, Maclaren had dimmed the fluoros around the observation deck, so that twilight filled it and the scientific apparatus crouched in ranks and on benches seemed to be a herd of long-necked monsters. Thus there was nothing to drown but the steely brilliance of the stars, when you looked out an unshuttered port.

*The* star hurtled across his field of view. Her eccentric orbit took the *Cross* around it in 37 minutes. Here, at closest approach, they were only half a million kilometers away. The thing had the visual diameter of three full Moons. It was curiously vague of outline: a central absolute blackness, fading toward deep gray near the edges where starlight caught an atmosphere more savagely compressed than Earth's ocean abyss. Through the telescope, there seemed to be changeable streaks and mottlings, bands, spots, a hint of color too faint for the eye to tell . . . as if the ghosts of burned-out fires still walked.

*Quite oblate,* Maclaren reminded himself. *That would have given us a hint, if we'd known. Or the radio spectrum; Now I realise, when it's too late, that the lines really are triplets, and their broadening is Doppler shift.*

The silence was smothering.

Nakamura drifted in. He poised himself in the air and waited quietly.

'Well?' said Maclaren.

'Sverdlov is still outside, looking at the accelerators and web,' said Nakamura. 'He will not admit there is no hope.'

'Neither will I,' said Maclaren.

'Virtually the whole system is destroyed. Fifty meters of it have vanished. The rest is fused, twisted, short-circuited . . . a miracle it continued to give some feeble kind of blast, so I could at least find an orbit.' Nakamura laughed. Maclaren thought that that high-pitched, apologetic giggle was going to be hard to live with, if one hadn't been raised among such symbols. 'We carry a few spare parts, but not that many.'

'Perhaps we can make some,' said Maclaren.

'Perhaps,' said Nakamura. 'But of course the accelerators are of no importance in themselves, the reconstruction of the web is the only way to get home. . . . What has the young man Ryerson to say about that?'

'Don't know. I sent him off to check the manifest and then look over the stuff the ship actually carries. He's been gone a long time, but –'

'I understand,' said Nakamura. 'It is not easy to face a death sentence when one is young.'

Maclaren nodded absently and returned his gaze to the scribbled data sheets in one hand. After a moment, Nakamura cleared his throat and said awkwardly, 'Ah . . . I beg your pardon . . . about the affair of Engineer Sverdlov –'

'Well?' Maclaren didn't glance up from the figures. He had a lot of composure of his own to win back. *The fact is,* he thought through a hammer-beat in his temples, *I am the man afraid. Now that there is nothing I can do, only a cold waiting until word is given me whether I can live or must die . . . I find that Terangi Maclaren is a coward.*

Sickness was a doubled fist inside his gullet.

'I am not certain what, er, happened,' stumbled Nakamura, 'and I do not wish to know. If you will be so kind . . . I hope you were not unduly inconvenienced –'

'No. It's all right.'

'If we could tacitly ignore it. As I think he has tried to do. Even the best men have a breaking point.'

*I always knew that there must one day be an end to white sails above green water, and to wine, and Nō masks, and a woman's laughter. I had not expected it yet.*

'After all,' said Nakamura, 'we must work together now.'

'Yes.' *I had not expected it a light-century from the home of my fathers. My life was spent in having fun, and now I find that the black star has no interest at all in amusing me.*

'Do you know yet what happened?' asks Nakamura. 'I would not press you for an answer, but –'

'Oh, yes,' said Maclaren. 'I know.'

Beneath a scraphead of songs and keels, loves and jokes and victories, which mattered no longer but would not leave him, Maclaren found his brain working with a startling dry clarity. 'I'm not sure how much we can admit to the others,' he said. 'Because this could have been averted, if we'd proceeded with more caution.'

'I wondered a little at the time.' Nakamura laughed again. 'But who would look for danger around a – a corpse?'

'Broadened spectrum lines mean a quickly rotating star,' said Maclaren. 'Since the ship was not approaching in the equatorial plane, we missed the full Doppler effect, but we might have stopped to think. And tripled lines mean a Zeeman splitting.'

'Ah.' Nakamura sucked in a hiss of air. 'Magnetism?'

'The most powerful bloody magnetic field ever noticed around any heavenly body,' said Maclaren. 'Judging from the readings I get here, the polar field is . . . oh, I can't say yet. Five, six, seven thousand gauss – somewhere on that order of magnitude. Fantastic! Sol's field is only 53 gauss. They don't ever go much above 2,000. Except here.'

He rubbed his chin. 'Blackett effect,' he went on. The steadiness of his words was a faintly pleasing surprise to him. 'Magnetic field is directly related to angular velocity.

The reason no live sun has a field like this dead thing here is that it would have to rotate too fast. Couldn't take the strain; it would go whoomp and scatter pieces of star from hell to tiffin.' An odd, perverse comfort in speaking lightly: a lie to oneself, persuading the subconscious mind that its companions were not doomed men and a black sun, but an amorous girl waiting for the next jest in a Citadel tavern. 'As this star collapsed on itself, after burning out, it had to spin faster, d'you see? Conservation of angular momentum: It seems to have had an unusual amount to start with, of course, but the rotational speed is chiefly a result of its degenerate state. And that same super-density allows it to twirl with such indecent haste. You might say the bursting strength is immensely greater.'

'Yes,' said Nakamura. 'I see.'

'I've been making some estimates,' said Maclaren. 'It didn't actually take a very strong field to wreck us. We could easily have been protected against it. Any ion-drive craft going close to a planet is – a counter-magnetic circuit with a feedback loop – elementary. But naturally, these big ships were not meant to land anywhere. They would certainly never approach a live sun this close, and the possibility of this black dwarf having such a vicious magnetism – well, no one ever thought of it.'

He shrugged. 'Figure it out yourself, Captain Nakamura. The old H, e, v formula. A proton traveling at three-fourths $c$ down a hundred-meter tube is deflected one centimeter by a field of seven one-hundredths gauss. We entered such a field at a million kilometers out, more or less. A tenuous but extremely energetic stream of ionised gas hit the outermost accelerator ring. I make the temperature equivalent of that velocity to be something like three million million degrees. Absolute, if I remember the value of the gas constant correctly. The closer to the star we got, the stronger field we were in, so the farther up the ions struck.

'Of course,' finished Maclaren in a tired voice, 'all these quantities are just estimates, using simple algebra. Since we slanted across the magnetic field, you'd need a vectorial differential equation to describe exactly what happened. You might find occasion to change my figures by a factor of five or six. But I think I have the general idea.'

'Yes-s-s,' said Nakamura, 'I think you do.'

They hung side by side in dimness and looked out at the eye-hurting bright stars.

'Do you know,' said Maclaren, 'there is one sin which is punished with unfailing certainty, and must therefore be the deadliest sin in all time. Stupidity.'

'I am not so sure.' Nakamura's reply jarred him a little, by its sober literal-mindedness. 'I have known many – well, shall I call them unintellectual? – people who lived happy and useful lives.'

'I wasn't referring to that kind of stupidity.' Maclaren went through the motions of a chuckle. 'I meant our own kind. Yours and mine. We bear the guilt, you know. We should have stopped and thought the situation over before rushing in. I did want to approach more slowly, measuring as we went, and you overruled me.'

'I am ashamed,' said Nakamura. He bent his face toward his hands.

'No, let me finish. I should have come here with a well-thought-out program in mind. I gave you no valid reasons *not* to establish a close-in orbit at once. My only grumble was that you wouldn't allow me time to take observations as we went toward the star. You were perfectly justified, on the basis of the information available to you – Oh, the devils take it! I bring this up only so you'll know what topics to avoid with our shipmates – who must also bear some of the blame for not thinking – because we can't afford quarrels.' Maclaren felt his cheeks crease in a sort of grin. 'I have no interest in the guilt question anyway. My problem is strictly pragmatic: I want out of here!'

Ryerson emerged from the living-quarter screen. Maclaren saw him first as a shadow. Then the young face came so near that he could see the eyes unnaturally bright and lips shaking.

'What have you found, Dave?' The question ripped from him before he thought.

Ryerson looked away from them both. Thickly: 'We can't do it. There aren't enough replacement parts to make a f-f-functioning . . . a web – we can't.'

'I knew that,' said Nakamura, 'Of course. But we have instruments and machine tools. There is bar metal in the hold, which we can shape to our needs. The only problem is – '

'Is where to get four kilos of pure germanium!' Ryerson screamed it. The walls sneered at him with echoes. 'Down on that star, maybe?'

# 9

SQUARE and inhuman in a spacesuit, Sverdlov led the way through the engine-room airlock. When Ryerson, following, stepped forth on to the ship's hull, there was a moment outside existence.

He snatched for his breath. Alien suns went streaming past his head. Otherwise he knew only blackness touched by meaningless dull splashes. He clawed after anything real. The motion tore him loose and he went spinning outward toward the dead star. But he felt it just as a tide of nausea; his ears roared at him, the scrambled darks and gleams made a wheel with himself crucified at the hub. He was never sure if he screamed.

The lifeline jerked him to a halt. He rebounded, more slowly. Sverdlov's sardonic voice struck his earphones, 'Don't be so jumpy next time, Earthling,' and there was a sense of direction as the Krasnan began to reel him in.

Suddenly Ryerson made out a pattern. The circle of shadow before him was the hull. The metallic shimmers projecting from it . . . oh, yes, one of the auxiliary tank attachments. The mass-ratio needed to reach one-half $c$ with an exhaust velocity of three-fourths $c$ is 4.35 – relativistic formulas apply rather than the simple Newtonian exponential – and this must be squared for deceleration. The *Cross* had left Sol with a tank of mercury on either side, feeding into the fuel deck. Much later, the empty containers had been knocked down into parts of the aircraft now stowed inboard.

Ryerson pulled his mind back from the snugness of

engineering data. Beyond the hull, and around it, behind him, for X billion light-years on all sides, lay the stars. The nearer ones flashed and glittered and stabbed his eyes, uncountably many. The outlines they scrawled were not those Ryerson remembered from Earth: even the recognisable constellations, like Sagittarius, were distorted, and he felt that as a somehow ghastly thing, as if it were his wife's face which had melted and run. The farther stars blended into the Milky Way, a single clotted swoop around the sky, the coldest color in all reality. And yet farther away, beyond a million light-years, you could see more suns – a few billions at a time, formed into the tiny blue-white coils of other galaxies.

Impact jarred Ryerson's feet. He stood erect, his boot-soles holding him by a weak stickiness to the plastic hull. There was just enough rotation to make the sky move slowly past his gaze. It created a dim sense of hanging head down; he thought of ghosts come back to the world like squeaking bats. His eyes sought Sverdlov's vague, armored shape. It was so solid and ugly a form that he could have wept his gratitude.

'All right,' grunted the Krasnan. 'Let's go.'

They moved precariously around the curve of the ship. The long thin frame-section lashed across their backs vibrated to their cautious footfalls. When they reached the lattice jutting from the stern, Sverdlov halted. 'Show you a trick,' he said. 'Light doesn't diffuse in vacuum, makes it hard to see an object in the round, so – ' He squeezed a small plastic bag with one gauntleted hand. His flashbeam snapped on, to glow through a fine mist in front of him. 'It's a heavy organic liquid. Forms droplets which hang around for hours before dissipating. Now, what d'you think of the transceiver web?'

Ryerson stooped awkwardly, scrambled about peering for several minutes, and finally answered: 'It bears out what you reported. I think all this can be repaired. But we'll have to take most of the parts inboard, perhaps melt them down – re-machine them, at least. And we'll need wholly new sections to replace what boiled away. Have we enough bar metal for that?'

'Guess so. Then what?'

'Then – ' Ryerson felt sweat form beneath his armpits and break off in little globs. 'You understand I am a graviticist, not a mattercasting engineer. A physicist would not be the best possible man to design a bridge; likewise, there's much I'll have to teach myself, to carry this out. But I can use the operating manual, and calculate a lot of quantities afresh, and . . . well . . . I think I could recreate a functioning web. The tuning will be strictly cut-and-try: you have to have exact resonance to get any effect at all, and the handbook assumes that such components as the distortion oscillator will have precise, standardised dimensions and crystal structure. Since they won't – we haven't the facilities to control it, even if I could remember what the quantities are – Well, once we've rebuilt what looks like a workable web, I'll have to try out different combinations of settings, perhaps for weeks, until . . . well, Sol or Centauri or . . . or any of the stations, even another spaceship . . . resonates – '

'Are you related to a Professor Broussard of Lomonosov Academy?' interrupted the other man.

'Why, no. What – '

'You lecture just like he used to. I am not interested in the theory and practice of mattercasting. I want to know, can we get home?'

Ryerson clenched a fist. He was glad that helmets and darkness hid their two face. 'Yes,' he said. 'If all goes well. And if we can find our four kilos of germanium.'

'What do you want that for?'

'Do you see those thick junction points in the web? They are, uh, you might call them giant transistors. Half the lattice is gone: there, the germanium was simply whiffed away. I do know the crystallo-chemical structure involved. And we can get the other elements needed by cannibalising, and there is an alloying unit aboard which could be adapted to manufacture the transistors themselves. But we don't have four spare kilos of germanium aboard.'

Sverdlov's tone grew heavy with skepticism, 'And that balloonhead Maclaren means to find a planet? And mine the stuff?'

'I don't know – ' Ryerson wet his lips. 'I don't know what else we can do.'

'But this star went supernova!'

'It was a big star. It would have had many planets. Some of the outermost ones – if they were large to start with – may have survived.'

'Ha! And you'd hunt around on a lump of fused nickel-iron, without even a sun in the sky, for germanium ore?'

'We have an isotope separator. It could be adapted to – I haven't figured it out yet, but – For God's sake!' Ryerson found himself screaming. 'What else can we do?'

'Shut up!' rasped Sverdlov. 'When I want my earphones broken I'll use a hammer.'

He stood in a swirl of golden fog, and the gray-rimmed black eye of the dead star marched behind him. Ryerson crouched back, hooked into the framework and waited. At last Sverdlov said, 'It's one long string of ifs. But a transistor doesn't do anything a vacuum tube can't.' He barked a laugh. 'And we've got all the vacuum we'll ever want. Why not design and make the equivalent electronic elements? Ought to be a lot easier than – repairing the accelerators, and scouring space for a planet.'

'Design them?' cried Ryerson. 'And test them, and redesign them, and – Do you realise that on half rations we have not quite six months' food supply?'

'I do,' said Sverdlov. 'I feel it in my belly right now.' He muttered a few obscenities. 'All right, then. I'll go along with the plan. Though if that clotbrain of a Nakamura hadn't – '

'He did the only thing possible! Did you *want* to crash us?'

'There are worse chances to take,' said Sverdlov. 'Now what have we got, but six months of beating our hearts out and then another month or two to die?' He made a harsh noise in the radiophone, as if wanting to spit. 'I've met Sarai settlers before. They're worse than Earthlings for cowardice, and nearly as stupid.'

'Now, wait – ' began Ryerson. 'Wait, let's not quarrel –'

'Afraid of what might happen?' jeered Sverdlov. 'You don't know your friend Maclaren's dirty-fighting tricks, do you?'

The ship whirled through a darkness that grew noisy with Ryerson's uneven breathing. He raised his hands against the bulky robot shape confronting him. 'Please,' he stammered. 'Now wait, wait, Engineer Sverdlov.' Tears stung his eyes. 'We're all in this together, you know.'

'I wondered just when you'd be coming up with that cliché,' snorted the Krasnan. 'Having decided it would be oh, so amusing to tell your society friends, how you spent maybe a whole month in deep space, you got me yanked off the job I really want to do, and tossed me into a situation you'd never once stopped to think about, and wrecked us all – and now you tell me, "We're all in this together"!' Suddenly he roared his words: 'You mangy son of a muck-eating cockroach, I'll get you back – not for your sake, nor for your wife's, because if she's an Earthling I know how she'll be spending the time you're gone – but for my own planet, d' you hear? They need me there!'

It grew very still. Ryerson felt how his heartbeat dropped down to normal, and then still further, until he could no longer hear his own pulse. His hands felt chilly and his face numb. A far and terrified part of him thought, *So this is how it feels, when the God of Hosts lays His hand upon a man,* but he stared past Sverdlov,

66

into the relentless white haze of the stars, and said in a flat voice: 'That will do. I've heard the story of the poor oppressed colonies before now. I think you yourself are proof that the Protectorate is better than you deserve. As for me, I never saw a milli of this supposed extortion from other planets: my father worked his way up from midshipman to captain, my brothers and I went through the Academy on merit, as citizens of the poorest and most overcrowded world in the universe. Do you imagine you know what competition is? Why, you blowhard clodhopper, you wouldn't last a week on Earth. As a matter of fact, I myself had grown tired of the struggle. If it weren't for this wretched expedition, my wife and I would have started for a new colony next week. Now you make me wonder if it's wise. Are all colonials like you – just barely brave enough to slander an old man and a woman when they're a safe hundred light-years away?'

Sverdlov did not move. The slow spin of the *Cross* bought the black star into Ryerson's view again. It seemed bigger, as the ship swooped toward periastron. He had a horrible sense of falling into it. *Thou, God, watchest me, with the cold ashen eye of wrath.* The silence was like a membrane stretched close to ripping.

Finally, very slow, the bass voice came. 'Are you prepared to back up those words, Earthling?'

'Right after we finish here!' shouted Ryerson.

'Oh.' A moment longer. Then, 'Forget it. Maybe I did speak out of turn. I've never known an Earthman who wasn't . . . an enemy of some kind.'

'Did you ever try to know them?'

'Forget it, I said. I'll get you home. I might even come around one day and say hello, on your new planet. Now let's get busy here. Our first job is to start the accelerators operating again.'

The weakness which poured through David Ryerson was such that he wondered if he would have fallen under gravity. *Oh, Tamara,* he thought, *be with me now.* He

remembered how they had camped on a California beach
. . . had it all to themselves, no one lived in the deserts
eastward . . . and the gulls had swarmed around begging
bread until both of them were helpless with laughter. Now
why should he suddenly remember that, out of all the
times they had had?

# 10

WHEN the mind gave up and the mathematics became a blur, there was work for Maclaren's hands. Sverdlov and Ryerson under him, did the machine-tool jobs; Nakamura's small fingers showed such delicacy that he was set to drawing wire and polishing control-ring surfaces. Maclaren was left with the least skilled assignment, least urgent because he was always far ahead of the consumption of his product: melting, separating, and re-alloying the fused salvage from ion accelerators and transceiver web.

But it was tricky in null-gee. There could not be any significant spin on the ship or assembly, out on the lattice, would have become too complicated for so small a gang of workers. Coriolis force would have created serious problems even for the inboard jobs. On the other hand, weightless melt had foul habits. Maclaren's left arm was still bandaged, the burn on his forehead still a crimson gouge.

It didn't seem to matter. When he looked in a mirror, he hardly recognised his face. There hadn't been much physical change yet, but the expression was a stranger's. And his life had narrowed to these past weeks, behind them lay only a dream. In moments when there was nothing else to do he might still play a quick chess game with Sverdlov, argue the merits of Nō versus Kabuki with Nakamura, or shock young Ryerson with a well-chosen dirty limerick. But thinking back, he saw how such times had become more and more sparse. He had quit trying to make iron rations palatable, when his turn in the galley came up; he had not sung a ballad for hundreds of the *Cross'* black-sun years. He shaved by the clock and hung on to fastidiousness of dress as pure ritual, the way Nakamura contemplated his paradoxes or Ryerson quoted his Bible or Sverdlov thumbed through his nude photographs of past mistresses. It was a way of telling yourself, *I am still alive.*

There came a moment when Maclaren asked himself what he was doing other than go through the motions of survival. That was a bad question.

'You see,' he told his mirror twin, 'it suggests a further inquiry: Why? And that's the problem we've been dodging all our mutual days.'

He stowed his electric razor, adjusted his tunic, and pushed out of the tiny bathroom. The living section was deserted, as it had been most of the time. Not only were they all too busy to sit around, but it was too narrow.

Outside its wall, he moved through the comfort of his instruments. He admitted frankly that his project of learning as much as possible of the star was three-quarters selfish. It was not really very probable that exact knowledge of its atmospheric composition would be of any use to their escape. But it offered him a chance, for minutes at a time, to forget where he was. Of course, he did not admit the fact to anyone but himself. And he wondered a little what reticences the other men had.

This time he was not alone. Nakamura hovered at an observation port. The pilot's body was outlined with unwavering diamond stars. But as the dead sun swung by, Maclaren saw him grow tense and bring a hand toward his eyes, as if to cover them.

He drifted soundlessly behind Nakamura. 'Boo,' he said.

The other whirled around in air, gasping. As the thresh of arms and legs died away, Maclaren looked upon terror.

'I'm sorry!' he exclaimed. 'I didn't think I'd startle you.'

'I . . . it is nothing.' Nakamura's brown gaze held some obscure beggary. 'I should not have – It is nothing.'

'Did you want anything of me?' Maclaren offered one of his last cigarettes. Nakamura accepted it blindly, without even saying thanks. *Something is very wrong with this lad,* thought Maclaren. Fear drained in through the glittering viewport. *And he's the only pilot we've got.*

'No. I had – I was resting a few moments. One cannot do precision work when . . . tired . . . yes-s-s.' Nakamura's hunger-gaunted cheeks caved in with the violence of his sucking on the tobacco. A little crown of sweat-beads danced about his head.

'Oh, you're not bothering me.' Maclaren crossed his legs and leaned back on the air. 'As a matter of fact, I'm glad of your company. I need someone to talk with.'

Nakamura laughed his meaningless laugh. 'We should look to you for help, rather than you to us,' he said. 'You are the least changed of us all.'

'Oh? I thought I was the most affected. Sverdlov hankers for his women and his alcohol and his politics. Ryerson wants back to his shiny new wife and his shiny new planet. You're the local rock of ages. But me – ' Maclaren shrugged. 'I've nothing to anchor me.'

'You have grown quieter, yes.' The cigarette in Nakamura's hand quivered a little, but his words came steadily now.

'I have begun to wonder about things.' Maclaren scowled at the black sun. By treating it as a scientific problem, he had held at arm's length the obsession he had seen eating at Ryerson – who grew silent and large-eyed and reverted to the iron religion he had once been shaking off – and at Sverdlov, who waxed bitterly profane. So far, Maclaren had not begun thinking of the star as a half-alive malignancy. But it would be all too easy to start.

'One does, sooner or later.' Nakamura's tone held no

71

great interest. He was still wrapped up in his private horror, and that was what Maclaren wanted to get him out of.

'But I don't wonder efficiently. I find myself going blank, when all I'm really doing is routine stuff and I could just as well be thinking at my problems.'

'Thought is a technique, to be learned,' said Nakamura, 'just as the uses of the body – ' He broke off. 'I have no right to teach. I have failed my own masters.'

'I'd say you were doing very well. I've envied you your faith. You have an answer.'

'Zen does not offer any cut-and-dried answers to problems. In fact, it tries to avoid all theory. No human system can comprehend the infinite real universe.'

'I know.'

'And that is my failure,' whispered Nakamura. 'I look for an explanation. I do not want merely to be. No, that is not enough . . . out here, I find that I want to be justified.'

Maclaren stared into the cruelty of heaven. 'I'll tell you something,' he said. 'I'm scared spitless.'

'What? But I thought – '

'Oh, I have enough flip retorts to camouflage it. But I'm as much afraid to die, I'm struggling as frantically and with as little dignity, as any trapped rat. And I'm slowly coming to see why, too. It's because I haven't got anything but my own life – my own minute meaningless life of much learning and no understanding, much doing and no accomplishing, many acquaintances and no friends – it shouldn't be worth the trouble of salvaging, should it? And yet I'm unable to see any more in the entire universe than just that: a lot of scurrying small accidents of organic chemistry, on a lot of flyspeck planets. If things made even a little sense, if I could see there was anything at all more important than this bunch of mucous membranes labeled Terangi Maclaren . . . why, then there'd be no reason to fear my own termination. The things that mattered would go on.'

Nakamura smoked in silence for a while. Maclaren finished his own cigarette in quick nervous puffs, fought temptation, swore to himself and lit another.

'I didn't mean to turn you into a weeping post,' he said. And he thought: *The hell I didn't. I fed you your psychological medicine right on schedule. Though perhaps I did make the dose larger than planned.*

'I am unworthy,' said Nakamura. 'But it is an honor.' He stared outward, side by side with the other man. 'I try to reassure myself with the thought that there must be beings more highly developed than we,' he said.

'Are you sure?' answered Maclaren, welcoming the chance to be impersonal. 'We've never found any that were even comparable to us. In the brains department, at least. I'll admit than Van Maanen's abos are more beautiful, and the Old Thothians more reliable and sweet-tempered.'

'How much do we know of the galaxy?'

'Um-m-m . . . yes.'

'I have lived in the hope of encountering a truly great race. Even if they are not like gods – they will have their own wise men. They will not look at the world just as we do. From each other, two such peoples could learn the unimaginable, just as the high epochs of Earth's history came when different peoples interflowed. Yes-s-s. But this would be so much more, because the difference is greater. Less conflict. What reason would there be for it? More to offer, a billion years of separate experience as life-forms.'

'I can tell you this much,' said Maclaren, 'the Protectorate would not like it. Our present civilisation couldn't survive such a transfusion of ideas.'

'Is our civilisation anything so great?' asked Nakamura with an unwonted scornfulness.

'No. I suppose not.'

'We have a number of technical tricks. Doubtless we could learn more from such aliens as I am thinking of. But what we would really learn that mattered – for

73

this era of human history lacks one – would be a philosophy.'

'I thought you didn't believe in philosophies.'

'I used a wrong word. I meant a $d\bar{o}$ – a way. A way of . . . an attitude? That is what life is for, that is your "Why" – it is not a mechanical cause-and-effect thing, it is the spirit in which we live.'

Nakamura laughed again. 'But hear the child correcting the master! I, who cannot even follow the known precepts of Zen, ask for help from the unknown! Were it offered me, I would doubtless crawl into the nearest worm-hole.'

And suddenly the horror flared up again. He grabbed Maclaren's arm. It sent them both twisting around, so that their outraged senses of balance made the stars whirl in their skulls. Maclaren felt Nakamura's grip like ice on his bare skin.

'I am afraid!' choked the pilot. 'Help me! I am afraid!'

They regained their floating positions. Nakamura let go and took a fresh cigaret with shaking fingers. The silence grew thick.

Maclaren said at last, not looking toward the Saraian, 'Why not tell me the reason? It might relieve you a bit.'

Nakamura drew a breath. 'I have always been afraid of space,' he said. 'And yet called to it also. Can you understand?'

'Yes. I think I know.'

'It has – ' Nakamura giggled ' – unsettled me. All my life. First, as a child I was taken from my home on Earth, across space. And now, of course, I can never come back.'

'I have some pull in the Citadel. A visa could be arranged.'

'You are very kind. I am not sure whether it would help. Kyoto cannot be as I remember it. If it has not changed, surely I have, yes-s-s? But please let me continue. After a few years on Sarai, there was a meteor fall which killed all my family except my brother. A stone

74

from space, do you see? We did not think of it that way, then. The monastery raised us. We got scholarships to an astronautical academy. We made a voyage together as cadets. Have you heard of the *Firdawzi* disaster?'

'No, I'm afraid not.' Maclaren poured smoke from his mouth, as a veil against the cosmos.

'Capella is a GO star like Sol, but a giant. The *Firdawzi* had been long at the innermost planet of the system, a remote-controlled survey trip. The radiations caused a metal fatigue. No one suspected. On our cruise, the ship suddenly failed. The pilot barely got us into an orbit, after we had fallen a long way toward Capella. There we had to wait until rescue came. Many died from the heat. My brother was one of them.'

Stillness hummed.

'I see,' said Maclaren at last.

'Since then I have been afraid of space. It rises into my consciousness from time to time.' Maclaren stole a glance at Nakamura. The little man was lotus-postured in midair, save that he stared at his hands and they twisted together. Wretchedness overrode his voice. 'And yet I could not stop my work either. Because out in space I often seem to come closer to . . . oneness . . . that which we all seek, what you have called understanding. But here, caught in this orbit about this star, the oneness is gone and the fear has grown and grown until I am afraid I will have to scream.'

'It might help,' said Maclaren.

Nakamura looked up. He tried to smile. 'What do you think?' he asked.

Maclaren blew a meditative cloud of smoke. Now he would have to pick his words with care – and no background or training in the giving of succor – or lose the only man who could pull this ship free. Or lose Nakamura: that aspect of it seemed, all at once, more important.

'I wonder,' he murmured, 'even in an absolutely free

75

society, if any such things could exist – I wonder if every man isn't afraid of his bride.'

'What?' Nakamura's lids snapped apart in startlement.

'And needs her at the same time,' said Maclaren. 'I might even extend it beyond sex. Perhaps fear is a necessary part of anything that matters. Could Bach have loved his God so magnificently without being inwardly afraid of Him? I don't know.'

He stubbed out his cigaret. 'I suggest you meditate upon this,' he said lightly. 'And on the further fact, which may be a little too obvious for you to have seen, that this is not Capella.'

Then he waited.

Nakamura made a gesture with his body. Only afterward, thinking about it, did Maclaren realise it was a free-fall prostration. 'Thank you,' he said.

'I should thank you,' said Maclaren, quite honestly. 'You gave me a leg up too, y'know.'

Nakamura departed for the machine shop.

Maclaren hung at the viewport a while longer. The rasp of a pocket lighter brought his head around.

Chang Sverdlov entered from the living section. The cigar in his mouth was held at a somehow resentful angle.

'Well,' said Maclaren, 'how long were you listening?'

'Long enough,' grunted the engineer.

He blew cheap, atrocious smoke until his pocked face was lost in it. 'So,' he asked, 'aren't you going to get mad at me?'

'If it serves a purpose,' said Maclaren.

'Uh!' Sverdlov fumed away for a minute longer. 'Maybe I had that coming,' he said.

'Quite probably. But how are the repairs progressing outside?'

'All right. Look here,' Sverdlov blurted, 'do me a favor, will you? If you can. Don't admit to Ryerson, or me, that you're human – that you're just as scared and confused as the rest of us. Don't admit it to Nakamura, even. You

76

didn't know, so far – not really. We need a – a – a damned cocky dude of a born-and-bred technic – to get us through!'

He whirled back into the quarters. Maclaren heard him dive, almost fleeing, aft along the shaft-way.

# 11

NAKAMURA noted in the log, which he had religiously maintained, the precise moment when the *Cross* blasted from the dead star. The others had not even tried to keep track of days. There were none out here. There was not even time, in any meaningful sense of the word – only existence, with an unreal impression of sunlight and leaves and women before existence began, like an inverted prenatal memory.

The initial minutes of blast were no more veritable. They took their posts and stared without any sense of victory at their instruments. Nakamura in the control turret, Maclaren on the observation deck feeding him data, Sverdlov and Ryerson watchful in the engine room, felt themselves merely doing another task in an infinite succession.

Sverdlov was the first who broke from his cold womb and knew himself alive. After an hour of poring over his dials and viewscreens, through eyes bulged by two gravities, he ran a hand across the bristles on his jaw. 'Holy fecal matter,' he whispered. 'The canine-descending thing is hanging together.'

And perhaps only Ryerson, who had worked outside with him for weeks of hours, could understand.

The lattice jutting from the sphere had a crude, unfinished look. And indeed little had been done toward restoring the transceiver web; time enough for that while they hunted a planet. Sverdlov had simply installed a framework to support his re-fashioned accelerator rings, antimagnetic shielding circuits, and incidental wire, tubes, grids, capacitors, transformers. . . . He had tested with a milliampere of ion current, cursed, readjusted, tested again, nodded, asked for a full amp, made obscene comments, readjusted, retested, and wondered if he could have done it without Ryerson. It was not so much that he needed the extra hands, but the boy had been impossibly patient. When Sverdlov could take no more electronic misbehavior, and went back into the ship and got a sledge and pounded at an iron bar for lack of human skulls to break, Ryerson had stayed outside trying a fresh hookup.

Once, when they were alone among galaxies, Sverdlov asked him about it. 'Aren't you human, kid? Don't you ever want to throw a rheostat across the room?'

Ryerson's tone came gnat-like in his earphones, almost lost in an endless crackling of cosmic noise. 'It doesn't do any good. My father taught me that much. We sailed a lot at home.'

'So?'

'The sea never forgives you.'

Sverdlov glanced at the other, couldn't find him in the tricky patching of highlight and blackness, and suddenly confronted Polaris. It was like being stabbed. How many men, he thought with a gasp, had followed the icy North Star to their weird?

'Of course,' Ryerson admitted humbly, 'it's not so easy to get along with people.'

And the lattice grew. And finally it tested sound, and Sverdlov told Nakamura they could depart.

The engine which had accelerated the *Cross* to half light speed could not lift her straight away from this sun. Nor could her men have endured a couple of hundred gravities, even for a short time. She moved out at two gees, her gyros holding the blast toward the mass she was escaping, so that her elliptical orbit became a spiral. It would take hours to reach a point where the gravitational field had dropped so far that a hyperbolic path would be practicable.

Sverdlov crouched in his harness, glaring at screens and indicators. The bloody damned dead cinder wasn't going to let them escape this easily! He had stared too long at its ashen face to imagine that. There would be some new trick, and he would have to be ready. God, he was thirsty! The ship did have a water-regenerating unit, merely because astronautical regulations at the time she was built insisted on it. Odd, owing your life to some bureaucrat two hundred years dust on his own filing cabinets. But the regenerator was inadequate and hadn't been used in all that time. No need for it: waste material went into the matter bank, and was reborn as water or food or anything else, according to a signal sent from the Lunar station with every change of watch.

But there were no more signals coming to the *Cross*. Food, once eaten, was gone for good. Recycled water was little more than enough to maintain life. *Fire and thunder!* thought Sverdlov. *I can smell myself two kilometers away. I might not sell out the Fellowship for a bottle of beer, but the Protector had better not offer me a case.*

A soft *brroom-brroom-brroom* pervaded his awareness, the engine talked to itself. Too loud, somehow. The instruments read okay, but Sverdlov did not think an engine with a good density would make so much noise. He glanced back at the viewscreens. The black sun was scarcely visible. It couldn't be seen at all unless you knew just where to look. The haywired ugliness of the ion drive made a cage for stars. The faintest blue glow wavered down the rings. Shouldn't, of course. Inefficiency. St. Elmo's fire danced near the after end of the assembly. 'Engine room to pilot. How are we making out?'

'Satisfactory.' Nakamura's voice sounded thin. It must be a strain, yes, he was doing a hundred things manually for which the ship lacked robots. But who could have anticipated – ?

Sverdlov narrowed his eyes. 'Take a look at the tail

of this rig, Dave,' he said. 'The rear negatron ring. See anything?'

'Well . . . ' The boy's eyes, dark-rimmed and blood-shot, went heavily after Sverdlov's pointing finger. 'Electrostatic discharge, that blue light – '

'See anything else?' Sverdlov glanced uneasily at the megammeters. He did not have a steady current going down the accelerators, it fluctuated continually by several per cent. But was the needle for the negatron side creeping ever so slowly downward?

'No. No, I can't.'

'Should'a put a thermocouple in every ring. Might be a very weak deflection of ions, chewing at the endmost till all at once its focusing goes blooey and we're in trouble.'

'But we tested every single – And the star's magnetic field is attenuating with every centimeter we advance.'

'Vibration, my cub-shaped friend. It'd be easy to shake one of those jury-rigged magnetic coils just enough out of alignment to – *Hold it!*'

The terminal starboard coil glowed red. Blue electric fire squirted forth and ran up the lattice. The negative megammeter dropped ten points and Sverdlov felt a little surge as the ship wallowed to one side from an unbalanced thrust.

'Engine room stopping blast!' he roared. His hand had already gone crashing on to the main lever.

The noise whined away to a mumble. He felt himself pitched off a cliff as high as eternity.

'What's the trouble?' barked Maclaren's voice.

Sverdlov relieved himself of a few unrepeatable remarks. 'Something's gone sour out there. The last negatron accelerator began to glow and the current to drop. Didn't you feel us yaw?'

'Oh, Lord, have mercy,' groaned Ryerson. He looked physically sick. 'Not again.'

'Ah, it needn't be so bad,' said Sverdlov. 'Me, I'm surprised the mucking thing held together this long. You

can't do much with baling wire and spit, you know.'
Inwardly, he struggled with a wish to beat somebody's
face.

'I presume we are in a stable orbit,' said Nakamura.
'But I would feel a good deal easier if the repair can be
made soon. Do you want any help?'

'No. Dave and I can handle it. Stand by to give us a
test blast.'

Sverdlov and Ryerson got into their spacesuits. 'I swear
this smells fouler every day,' said the Krasnan. 'I didn't
believe I could be such a filth generator.' He slapped
down his helmet and added into the radio: 'So much for
man the glorious star-conqueror.'

'No,' said Ryerson.

'What?'

'The stinks are only the body. That isn't important.
What counts is the soul inside.'

Sverdlov cocked his bullet head and stared at the
other armored shape. 'Do you actually believe that guff?'

'I'm sorry, I didn't mean to preach or – '

'Never mind. I don't feel like arguing either.' Sverdlov
laughed roughly. 'I'll give you just one thing to mull over,
though. If the body's such a valueless piece of pork, and
we'll all meet each other in the sweet bye and bye, and
so on, why're you busting every gut you own to get back
to your wife?'

He heard an outraged breath in his earphones. For a
moment he felt he had failed somehow. There was no
room here for quarrels. *Ah, shaft it,* he told himself. *If an
Earthling don't like to listen to a colonial, he can jing-
bangle well stay out of space.*

They gathered tools and instruments in a silence that
smoldered. When they left the airlock, they had the usual
trouble in seeing. Then their pupils expanded and their
minds switched over to the alien gestalt. A raw blaze
leaped forth and struck them.

Feeling his way aft along the lattice, Sverdlov sensed
his anger bleed away. The boy was right – it did no good

to curse dead matter. Save your rage for those who needed it, tyrants and knaves and their sycophants. And you might even wonder (it was horrible to think) if they were worth it either. He stood with ten thousand bitter suns around him; but none were Sol or Tau Ceti. O Polaris, death's lodestar, are we as little as all that?

He reached the end of the framework, clipped his life-line on, and squirted a light-diffusing fog at the ring. Not too close, he didn't want it to interfere with his ion stream, but it gave him three-dimensional illumination. He let his body float out behind while he pulled himself squinting-close to the accelerator.

'Hm, yes, it's been pitted,' he said. 'Naturally it would be the negatron side which went wrong. Protons do a lot less harm, striking terrene matter. Hand me that counter, will you?'

Ryerson, wordless and faceless, gave him the instrument. Sverdlov checked for radioactivity. 'Not enough to matter,' he decided. 'We won't have to replace this ring, we stopped the process in time. By readjusting the magnetic coils we can compensate for the change in the electric focusing field caused by its gnawed-up shape. I hope.'

Ryerson said nothing. *Good grief*, thought Sverdlov, *did I offend him that much?* Hitherto they had talked a little when working outside, not real conversation but a trivial remark now and then, a grunt for response . . . just enough to drown out the hissing of the stars.

'Hello, pilot. Give me a microamp. One-second dura-tion.'

Sverdlov moved out of the way. Even a millionth of an ampere blast should be avoided, if it was an antiproton current.

Electric sparks crawled like ivy over the bones of the accelerator. Sverdlov, studying the instruments he had planted along the ion path, nodded. 'What's the poten-tiometer say, Dave?' he asked. 'If it's saying anything fit to print, I mean.'

'Standard,' snapped Ryerson.

*Maybe I should apologise,* thought Sverdlov. And then, in a geyser: *Judas, no! If he's so thin-skinned as all that, he can rot before I do.*

The stars swarmed just out of reach. Sometimes changes in the eyeball made them seem to move. Like flies. A million burning flies. Sverdlov swatted, unthinkingly, and snarled to himself.

After a while it occurred to him that Ryerson's nerves must also be rubbed pretty thin. You shouldn't expect the kid to act absolutely sensibly. *I lost my own head at the very start of this affair,* thought Sverdlov. The memory thickened his temples with blood. He began unbolting the Number One magnetic coil as if it were an enemy to emasculate.

'Okay, gimme another microamp one-second test.'

'Try shifting Number Two a few centimeters forward,' said Ryerson.

'You crazy?' snorted Sverdlov. *Yes, I suppose we're all a bit crazy by now.* 'Look, if the deflected stream strikes here, you'll want to bend it down like so and – '

'Never mind.' Ryerson could not be seen to move, in the bulk of his armor, but Sverdlov imagined him turning away with a contemptuous shrug. It took several minutes of tinkering for the Krasnan to realise that the Earthling had visualised the interplay of forces correctly.

He swallowed. 'You were right,' he emitted.

'Well, let's get it reassembled,' said Ryerson coldly.

*Very good, Earth snob, sir.* Sverdlov attacked the coils for several more minutes. 'Test blast.' Not quite. Try another setting. 'Test blast. Repeat.' That seemed to be it. 'Give me a milliamp this time. . . . A full amp . . . hm-m.' The current had flowed too short a time to heat the ring, but needles wavered wildly.

'We're still getting some deflection,' said Sverdlov. 'Matter of velocity distribution. A certain small percentage of the particles have abnormal velocities and – ' He realised he was crouched under Ryerson's hidden eyes babbling the obvious. 'I'll try sliding this one a wee bit more aside. Gimme that vernier wrench. . . . So. One amp test blast, please.'

There was no further response from the instruments. Ryerson let out a whistling sigh. 'We seem to have done it,' he said.

*We?* thought Sverdlov. *Well, you handed me a few tools!*

Aloud: 'We won't know for sure till full thrust is applied.'

'Of course,' Ryerson spoke hesitantly. Sverdlov recognised the tone, it was trying to be warm. Ryerson was over his fit of temper.

*Well, I'm not!*

'There isn't anything to be done about that except to try it and see, is there,' went on the Earthling.

'And if we still get significant deflection, drag on our suits and crawl back here – maybe a dozen times? No!'

'Why, that was how we did it before.'

'I'm getting awfully hungry,' said Sverdlov. Suddenly it flared out of him. 'I'm sick of it! I'm sick of being cooped up in my own stink, and yours, I'm sick of the same stupid faces and the same stupid remarks, yes, the same stars even! I've had enough! Get on back inside. I'll stay here and watch under acceleration. If anything goes wrong, I'll be right on the spot to fix it.'

'But – '

Nakamura's voice crackled above the mutter of stars. 'What are you thinking of, Engineer Sverdlov? Two gravities would pull you off the ship! And we're not maneuvrable enough to rescue you.'

'This lifeline is tested for two thousand kilos,' said the Krasnan. 'It's standard procedure to make direct high-acceleration checks on the blast.'

'By automatic instruments.'

'Which we haven't got. Do you *know* the system is fully adjusted? Are you so sure there isn't some small cumulative effect, so the thing will quit on you one day when you need it the most?'

Maclaren's tone joined in, dry and somehow remote, 'This is a curious time to think about that.'

'I am the engineer,' said Sverdlov stiffly. 'Read the ship's articles again.'

'Well,' said Nakamura. 'Well, but –'

'It would save time,' said Ryerson. 'Maybe even a few days' worth of time, if the coils really are badly maladjusted.'

'Thanks, Dave,' said Sverdlov clumsily.

'Well,' said Nakamura, 'you have the authority, of course. But I ask you again –'

'All I ask of *you* is two gravities' worth of oof for a few seconds,' interrupted Sverdlov. 'When I'm satisfied this ring will function properly, so we won't have to be forever making stops like this, I'll come inside.'

He hooked his legs about the framework and began resetting the instruments clamped on to it. 'Get on back, Dave,' he said.

'Why ... I thought I would –'

'No need to.'

'But there is! You can't read every dial simultaneously, and if there's work to be done you'll need help.'

'I'll call you if I want you. Give me your tool belt.' Sverdlov took it from reluctant hands and buckled it around himself. 'There is a certain amount of hazard involved, Dave. If I should be unlucky, you're the closest approximation to an engineer the ship will have. She can't spare both of us.'

'But why take any risk at all?'

'Because I'm sick of being here! Because I've got to fight back at that damned black coal or start howling! Now get inside!'

As he watched the other blocky shape depart him, Sverdlov thought: *I am actually not being very rational, am I now? But who could expect it, a hundred light-years from the sun?*

As he made ready, he puzzled over what had driven

him. There was the need to wrestle something tangible; and surely to balance on this skeleton of metal, under twice his normal weight, was a challenge. Beyond that, less important really, was the logic of it: the reasons he had given were sound enough as far as they went, and you could starve to death while proceeding at the pace of caution.

And below it all, he thought, was a dark wish he did not understand. Li-Tsung of Krasna would have told him to live at all costs, sacrifice all the others, to save himself for his planet and the Fellowship. But there were limits. You didn't have to accept Dave's Calvinism – though its unmerciful God seemed very near this dead star – to swallow the truth that some things were more important than survival. Than even the survival of a cause.

*Maybe I'm trying to find out what those things are,* he thought confusedly.

He crawled 'up' till his feet were braced on a cross-member, with the terminal accelerator ring by his right ankle but the electroprober dial conveniently near his faceplate. His right hand gripped a vernier wrench, his left drew taut the lifeline. 'Stand by for blast,' he said into his radio. 'Build up to two gees over a one-minute period, then hold it till I say cut.'

Nothing happened for a while except the crawling of the constellations at gyros brought the ship around. Good boy, Seiichi! He'd get some escape distance out of even a test blast. 'Stand by,' it said in Sverdlov's earphones. And his weight came back to him, until he felt an exultant straining in the muscles of shoulder and arm and leg and belly; until his heart thudded loud enough to drown out the thin crackling talk of the stars.

The hull was above him now, a giant sphere upheld on twin derricks. Down the middle of each derrick guttered a ghostly blue light, and sparks writhed and fountained at junction points. The constellations shone chill through the electric discharge.

87

*Inefficient*, thought Sverdlov. *The result of reconstruction without adequate instruments. But it's pretty. Like festival fireworks.* He remembered a pyrotechnic display once, when he was small. His mother had taken him. They sat on a hired catamaran and watched wonder explode softly above the lake.

'Uh,' grunted Sverdlov. He narrowed his eyes to peer at the detector dial. There certainly was a significant deflection yet, when whole grams of matter were being thrown out every second. It didn't heat up the ring very much, maybe not enough to notice; but negatrons plowed through terrene electron shells, into terrene nuclei, and atoms were destroyed. Presently there would be crystal deformation, fatigue, ultimate failure. He reported his findings and added with a sense of earned boasting: 'I was right. This had to be done.'

'I shall halt blast, then. Stand by.'

Weightlessness came back. Sverdlov reached out delicately with his wrench, nipped a coil nut, and loosened the bolt. He shifted the coil itself backward. 'I'll have this fixed in a minute. There! Now give me three gees for about thirty seconds, just to make sure.'

'Three? Are you certain you –'

'I am. Fire!'

It came to Sverdlov that this was another way a man might serve his planet: just by being the right kind of man. Maybe a better way than planning the extinction of people who happened to live somewhere else. *Oh, come off it,* he told himself, *next thing you'll be teaching a Humane League kindergarten.*

The force on him climbed, and his muscles rejoiced in it.

At three gees there was no deflection against the ring . . . or was there? He peered closer. His right hand, weighted by the tool it still bore, slipped from the member on which it had been leaning. Sverdlov was thrown off balance. He flung both arms wide, instinctively trying not

88

to fall. His right went between the field coils and into the negatron stream.

Fire spouted.

Nakamura cut the drive. Sverdlov hung free, staring by starlight at his arm. The blast had sliced it across as cleanly as an industrial torch. Blood and water vapor rushed out and froze in a small cloud, pale among the nebulae.

There was no pain. Not yet. But his eardrums popped as pressure fell. 'Engine room!' he snapped. A part of him stood aside and marveled at his own mind. What a survival machine, when the need came! 'Emergency! Drop total accelerator voltage to one thousand. Give me about ten amps down the tube. Quick!'

He felt no weight, such a blast didn't exert enough push on the hull to move it appreciably. He thrust his arm back into the ion stream. Pain did come now, but in his head, as the eardrums ruptured. One minute more and he would have the bends. The gas of antiprotons roared without noise around the stump of his wrist. Steel melted. Sverdlov prodded with a hacksaw gripped in his left hand, trying to seal the spacesuit arm shut.

He seemed far away from everything. Night ate at his brain. He asked himself once in wonderment. 'Was I planning to do this to other men?'

When he thought the sleeve was sealed, he withdrew it. 'Cut blast,' he whispered. 'Come and get me.' His air-tanks fed him oxygen, pressure climbed again inside the suit. It was good to float at the end of a lifeline, breathing. Until he began to strangle on his own blood. Then he gave up and accepted the gift of darkness.

# 12

Now, about winter solstice, day was a pale glimmer, low in the south among steel-colored clouds. Tamara had been walking since the first light sneaked across the ocean, and already the sun was close to setting. She wondered if space itself could be blacker than this land. At least you saw the stars in space. On Skula you huddled indoors against the wind, and the sky was a blind whirl of snow.

A few dry flakes gusted as she came down off the moor to the beach. But they carried no warmth with them, there was not going to be a snowfall tonight. The wind streaked in from a thousand kilometers of Atlantic and icebergs. She felt the cold snap its teeth together around her; a hooded cloak was small protection. But she *would* not go back to the house. Not till day had drained from the world and it would be unsafe to remain outdoors.

She said to herself, drearily: *I would stay here even then, except it might harm the child, and the old man would come looking for me. David, help me, I don't know which would be worse!*

There was a twisted pleasure in being so honest with herself. By all the conventions, she should be thinking only of David's unborn baby, herself no more than its vessel. But it was not real to her . . . not yet . . . so far it was only sickness in the mornings and bad dreams at night. The reality was Magnus Ryerson, animal-like hairiness and a hoarse grumble at her for not doing the housework his way and incomprehensible readings aloud

– his island and his sea and his bloody damned language lessons!

Tamara found herself voicing the curses. 'Bloody damned English! Bloody damned English! You can take your language and you know what you can do with it!' She had heard the expression now and then – overheard it, rather, as a small girl peeping through doors while men talked – some of the coarser sort used such phrases, fish ranchers or coral miners or cattle guards. She was not sure what it was everybody knew could be done with it. Tear it into little bits, probably, and fling it on the wind, into the ugly Northern ocean.

For a moment her hands clawed together. If she could so destroy Magnus Ryerson!

She fought for decorum. She was a lady. Not a technic, but still a professor's daughter; she could read and write, she had learned to dance and play the flute, pour tea and embroider a dress and converse with learned men so they were not too bored while waiting for her father . . . the arts of graciousness. Her father would call it contrasocial, to hate her husband's father. This was her family now.

But.

Her boots picked a way down the hillside, through snow and heather bushes, until she came out on a beach of stones. The sea came directly in here, smashing at heaped boulders with a violence that shivered through the ground. She saw how the combers exploded where they struck. Spindrift stung her skin. Beyond the rocks was only a gray waste of galloping white-bearded waves, and the wind keening down from the Pole, It rolled and boomed and whistled out there.

She remembered a living greenish blue of southern waters, how they murmured up to the foot of palm trees under infinitely tall skies.

She remembered David saying wryly: 'My people were Northerners as far back as we can trace it – Picts, Norse, Scots, sailors and crofters on the Atlantic edge – that must be why so many of them have become spacemen in the last several generations. To get away!'

And then, touching her hair with his lips, 'But I've found what all of them were really looking for.'

It was hard to imagine that David's warmth and tenderness and laughter had arisen in this tomb of a country. She had always thought of the religion which so troubled him (he first came to know her through her father, professor and student had sat up many nights under Australian stars while David groped for a God not all iron and hellfire) as an alien stamp, as if the legendary Other Race Out There had once branded him. The obscurity of the sect had aided her: Christians were not uncommon even today, but she had vaguely imagined a Protestant was some kind of Moslem.

Now she saw that Skula's dwellers and Skula's God had come from Skula itself, with winter seas in their veins. David had not been struggling toward normality; he had been reshaping himself into something which – down underneath – Magnus Ryerson thought was not human. Suddenly, almost blindingly, Tamara remembered a few weeks ago, one night when the old man had set her a ballad to translate. 'Our folk have sung it for many hundreds of years,' he said – and how he had looked at her under his heavy brows.

> *He hath taken off cross and iron helm,*
> *He hath bound his good horse to a limb,*
> *He hath not spoken Jesu name*
> *Since the Faerie Queen did first kiss him.'*

Tamara struck a fist into one palm. The wind caught her cloak and peeled it from her, so that it flapped at her shoulders like black wings. She pulled it back around her, shuddering.

The sun was a red sliver on the world's rim. Darkness would come in minutes, so thick you could freeze to death fumbling your way home. Tamara began to walk, quickly, hoping to find a decision. She had not come out today just because the house was unendurable. But her mind had been stiff, as if rusted. She still didn't know what to do.

*Or rather,* she thought, *I do know, but haven't saved up enough courage.*

When she reached the house, the air was already so murky she could almost not make out whitewashed walls and steep snow-streaked roof. A few yellow gleams of light came through cracks in the shutters. She paused at the door. To go in – ! But there was no choice. She twisted the knob and stepped through. The wind and the sea-growl came in with her.

'Close the door,' said Magnus. 'Close the door, you little fool.'

She shut out all but a mumble and whine under the eaves, hung her cloak on a peg and faced around. Magnus Ryerson sat in his worn leather chair with a worn leather-bound book in his hands. As always, as always! How could you tell one day from the next in this den? The radiglobe was turned low, so that he was mostly shadow, with an icicle gleam of eyes and the dirty-white cataract of beard. A peat fire sputtered forlornly, trying to warm a teakettle on the hob.

Ryerson put the book down on his lap, knocked out his archaic pipe (it had made the air foul in here) and asked roughly, 'Where have you been all day, girl? I was about to go look for you. You could turn an ankle and die of exposure, alone on the ling.'

'I didn't,' said Tamara. She exchanged her boots for zori and moved toward the kitchen.

'Wait!' said Magnus. 'Will you never learn? I want my high tea at just 1630 hours. . . . Now. You must be more careful, lass. You're carrying the last of the Ryersons.'

Tamara stopped. There was a downward slant to the ancient brick floor, she felt vaguely how her body braced itself. More nearly she felt how her chilled skin,

93

which had begun to tingle as it warmed, grew numb again.

'Besides David,' she said.

'If he is alive. Do you still believe it, after all these weeks?' Magnus began scraping out his pipe. He did not look at her.

'I don't believe he is dead,' she answered.

'The Lunar crew couldn't establish grav-beam contact. Even if he is still alive, he'll die of old age before that ship reaches any star where men have an outpost. No, say rather he'll starve!'

'If he could repair whatever went wrong – '

The muffled surf-drums outside rolled up to a crescendo. Magnus tightened his mouth. 'That is one way to destroy yourself . . . hoping,' he said. 'You must accept the worst, because there is always more of the worst than the best in this universe.'

She glanced at the black book he called a Bible, heavy on one of the crowded shelves. 'Do your holy writings claim that?' she asked. Her voice came out as a stranger's croak.

'Aye. So does the second law of thermodynamics.' Magnus knocked his pipe against the ashtray. It was an unexpectedly loud noise above the wind.

'And you . . . and you . . . won't even let me put up his picture,' she whispered.

'It's in the album, with my other dead sons. I'll not have it on the wall for you to blubber at. Our part is to take what God sends us and still hold ourselves up on both feet.'

'Do you know – ' Tamara stared at him with a slowly rising sense of horror. 'Do you know, I cannot remember just what he looked like?'

She had had some obscure hope of provoking his rage. But the shaggy-sweatered broad shoulders merely lifted, a little shrug. 'Aye, that's common enough. You've the words, blonde hair and blue eyes and so on, but they make not any real image. Well, you didn't know him so very long, after all.'

*You are telling me I am a foreigner,* she thought. *An interloper who stole what didn't belong to me.*

'There's time to review a little English grammar before tea,' said the old man. 'You've been terrible with the irregular verbs.'

He put his book on the table – she recognised the title, Kipling's poems, whoever Kipling had been – and pointed at a shelf. 'Fetch the text and sit down.'

Something flared in the girl. She doubled her fists. 'No.'

'What?' The leather face turned in search of her.

'I am not going to study any more English.'

'No – ' Magnus peered as if she were a specimen from another planet. 'Don't you feel well?'

She bit off the words, one after another: 'I have better ways to spend my time than learning a dead language.'

'Dead?' cried the man. She felt his rage lift in the air between them. 'The language of fifty million – '

'Fifty million ignorant provincials, on exhausted lands between bombed-out cities,' she said. 'You can't step outside the British Isles or a few pockets on the North American coast and have it understood. You can't read a single modern author or scientist or . . . or anybody . . . in English. I say it's dead! A walking corpse!'

'Your own husband's language!' he bawled at her, half rising.

'Do you think he ever spoke it to anyone but you, once he'd . . . he'd escaped?' she flung back. 'Did you believe . . . if David ever returns from that ship you made him go on . . . and we go to Rama – did you imagine we'd speak the language of a dying race? On a new world?'

She felt the tears as they whipped down her face, she gulped after breath amidst terror. The old man was so hairy, so huge. When he stood up, the single radiglobe and the wan firelight threw his shadow across her and

95

choked a whole corner of the room with it. His head bristled against the ceiling.

'So now your husband's race is dying,' he said like a gun. 'Why did you marry him, if he was that effete?'

'*He* isn't!' she called out. The walls wobbled around her. 'You are! Sitting here in your dreams of the past, when your people ruled Earth – a past we're well out of! David was going where . . . where the future is!'

'I see.' Magnus Ryerson turned half away from her. He jammed both fists into his pockets, looked down at the floor and rumbled his words to someone else – not her.

'I know. You're like the others, brought up to hate the West because it was once your master. Your teacher. The white man owned this planet a few centuries ago. Our sins then will follow us for the next thousand years . . . till your people fail in their turn, and the ones you raised up take revenge for the help they got. Well, I'm not going to apologise for my ancestors. I'm proud of them. We were no more vicious than any other men, and we gave . . . even on the deathbed of our civilisation, we gave you the stars.'

His voice rose until it roared. 'And we're not dead yet! Do you think this miserable Protectorate is a society? It isn't! It's not even a decent barbarism. It's a glorified garrison. It's the one worshiping the status quo and afraid to look futureward. I went to space because my people once went to sea. I gave my sons to space, and you'll give yours to space, because that's where the next civilisation will be! And you'll learn the history and the language of our people – your people – by God, you'll learn what it *means* to be one of us!'

His words rang away into emptiness. For a while only the wind and a few tiny flames had voice. Down on the strand, the sea worried the island like a terrier with a rat.

Tamar said finally, 'I already know what it means. It cost me David, but I know.'

He faced her again, lowered his head and stared as if at an enemy.

'You murdered him,' she said, not loudly. 'You sent him to a dead sun to die. Because you –'

'You're overwrought,' he broke in with tight-held anger. 'I urged him to try just one space expedition. And this one was important. It could have meant a deal to science. He would have been proud afterward, whatever he did for a career, to say, "I was on the *Cross*." '

'So he should die for his pride?' she said. 'It's as senseless a reason as the real one. But I'll tell you why you really made him go . . . and if you deny you forced him, I'll say you lie! You couldn't stand the idea that one child of yours had broken away – was not going to be wrenched into your image – had penetrated this obscene farce of space exploration, covering distance for its own sake, as if there were some virtue in a large number of kilometers. David was going to live as nature meant him to live, on a living soil, with untanked air to breathe and with mountains to walk on instead of a spinning coffin . . . and his children would too . . . we would have been happy! And that was what you couldn't stand to have happen!'

Magnus grinned without humor. 'There's a lot of meaningless noise for a symbolics professor's daughter to make,' he said. 'To begin at the end, what proof have you we were meant to be happy?'

'What proof have you we were meant to jump across light-years?' she cried. 'It's another way of running from yourself – no more. It's not even a practical thing. If the ships only looked for planets to colonise, I could understand. But . . . the *Cross* herself was aimed for three giants! She was diverted to a black clinker! And now David is dead . . . for what? Scientific curiosity? You're not a research scientist, neither was he, and you know it. Wealth? He wasn't being paid more than he could earn on Earth. Glory? Few enough people on Earth care about exploration; not many more on Rama; he, not at all. Adventure? You can have more adventure in an hour's walk through a forest than in a year on a spaceship. I say you murdered your son because you saw him becoming sane!'

'Now that's enough,' growled Magnus. He took a step toward her. 'I've heard enough out of you. In my own house. And I never did hold with this new-fangled notion of letting a woman yap – '

'Stand back!' she yelled. 'I'm not *your* wife!'

He halted. The lines in his face grew suddenly blurred. He raised his artificial hand as if against a blow.

'You're my son's wife,' he said, quite gently. 'You're a Ryerson too ... now.'

'Not if this is what it means.' She had found the resolution she sought. She went to the wall and took her cloak off its peg. 'You'll lend me your aircar for a hop to Stornoway, I trust. I will send it back on auto-pilot and get transport for myself from there.'

'But where are you going?' His voice was like a hurt child's.

'I don't know,' she snapped. 'To some place with a bearable climate. David's salary is payable to me till he's declared dead, and then there will be a pension. When I've waited long enough to be sure he won't come back, I'm going to Rama.'

'But, lass – propriety – '

'Propriety be damned. I'd rather have David's child, alive.'

She slipped her boots back on, took a flashlight from the cupboard, and went out the door. As she opened it, the wind came straight in and hit Magnus across the face.

*'In the land of Chinchanchou,*
   *Where the winds blow tender*
*From a sea like purple wine*
   *Foaming to defend her,*
*Lives a princess beautiful*
   *(May the gods amend her!)*
*Little known for virtue, but*
   *Of most female gender.'*

As HE came around the gyro housing and pulled himself forward to the observation deck, David Ryerson heard the guitar skitter through half a dozen chords and Maclaren's voice come bouncing in its wake. He sighed, pushed the lank yellow hair back out of his eyes, and braced himself.

Maclaren floated in the living section. It was almost an insult to see him somehow clean all over, in a white tunic, when each man was allowed a daily spongeful of water for such purposes. And half rations had only leaned the New Zealander down, put angles in his smooth brown countenance; he didn't have bones jutting up under a stretched skin like Ryerson, or a flushed complexion and recurring toothache like Nakamura. It wasn't fair!

'Oh, hullo, Dave.' Maclaren continued tickling his strings, but quietly. 'How does the web progress?'

'I'm done.'

'Hm?'

'I just clinched the last bolt and spotwelded the last

connection. There's not a thing left except to find that germanium, make the transistors, and adjust the units.' Ryerson hooked an arm around a stanchion and drifted free, staring out of sunken eyes toward emptiness. 'God help me,' he murmured, 'what am I going to do now?'

'Wait,' said Maclaren. 'We can't do much except wait.' He regarded the younger man for a while. 'Frankly, both Seiichi and I found excuses not to help you, did less out there than we might have, for just that reason. I've been afraid you would finish the job before we found our planet.'

Ryerson started. Redness crept into his chalky face. 'Why, of all the – ' His anger collapsed. 'I see. All right.'

'These weeks since we escaped have been an unparalleled chance to practice my music,' remarked Maclaren. 'I've even been composing. Listen.

*'In their golden-masted ships*
  *Princes come a-wooing*
*Over darkling spindrift roads*
  *Where the gales are brewing.*
*Lusty tales have drawn them thence,*
  *Much to their undoing:*
*When they seek the lady's hand*
  *She gives them the —'*

'Will you stop that?' screamed Ryerson.

'As you like,' said Maclaren mildly. He put the guitar back into its case. 'I'd be glad to teach you,' he offered.

'No.'

'Care for a game of chess?'

'No.'

'I wish to all the hells I'd been more of an intellectual,' said Maclaren. 'I never was, you know. I was a playboy, even in science. Now . . . I wish I'd brought a few hundred books with me. When I get back, I'm going to read them.' His smile faded. 'I think I might begin to understand them.'

100

'When we get back?' Ryerson's thin frame doubled in mid air as if for a leap. '*If* we get back, you mean!'

Nakamura entered. He had a sheaf of scribbled papers in one hand. His face was carefully blank. 'I have completed the calculations on our latest data,' he said.

Ryerson shuddered. 'What have you found?' he cried. 'For God's sake, what have you found?'

'Negative.'

'Lord God of Israel,' groaned Ryerson. 'Negative again.'

'That pretty well covers this orbit, then,' said Maclaren calmly. 'I've got the elements of the next one computed – somewhere.' He went out among the instruments.

A muscle in Ryerson's cheek began to jump of itself. He looked at Nakamura for a long time. 'Isn't there anything else we can do?' he asked. 'The telescopes, the – Do we just have to *sit*?'

'We are circling a dead sun,' the pilot reminded him. 'There is only feeble starlight to see by. A very powerful instrument might photograph a planet, but not the telescopes we have. Not at any distance greater than we could find them gravitationally. S-s-so.'

'We could make a big telescope!' exclaimed Ryerson. 'We have glass, and . . . and silver and –'

'I've thought of that.' Maclaren's tones drifted back from the observation section. 'You're welcome to amuse yourself with it, but we'd starve long before a suitable mirror could be ground with the equipment here.'

'But – Maclaren, space is so big! We could hunt for a million years and never find a planet if we can't . . . can't see them!'

'We're not working quite at random.' Maclaren reappeared with a punched tape. 'Perhaps you've forgotten the principle on which we are searching. We establish ourselves in an orbit about the star, follow it for a while, check our position repeatedly, and compute whether the path has been significantly perturbed. If it has been, that's due to a planet somewhere, and we can do a Leverrier to find that planet. If not – if we're too far away – we quarter to another arc of the same path and try again. Having exhausted a whole circumference thus, we move outward and try a bigger circle.'

'Shut up!' rasped Ryerson. 'I know it! I'm not a school-boy, damn you! But we're *guessing*!'

'Not quite,' said Maclaren. 'You were occupied with the web when I worked out the secondary principle . . . yes, come to think of it, you never did ask me before. Let me explain. You see, by extrapolating from data on known stellar types, I know approximately what this star was like in its palmy days. From this, planetary-formation theory gives me the scale of its one-time system. For instance, its planets must have been more or less in the equatorial plane; such quantities as mass, angular momentum, and magnetic field determine the Bode's Law constants; to the extent that all this is known, I can draw an orbital map.

'Well, then the star went supernova. Its closer planets were whiffed into gas. The outermost giants would have survived, though badly damaged. But the semi-major axes of their orbits were so tremendous – theoretically, planets could have formed as much as a light-year from this star – that even a small percentage of error in the data makes my result uncertain by Astronomical Units. Another factor: the explosion filled this space with gas. We're actually inside a nonluminous nebula. That would shorten the orbits of the remaining planets; in the course of millions of years they've spiraled far inward. In one way that helps us: we've an area to search which is not hopelessly huge. But on the other hand, just how long has it been since the accident? What's the density dis-tribution of the nebula now, and what was it back then? I've taken some readings and made some estimates. All very crude, but – ' Maclaren shrugged – 'what else can we do? The successive orbits we have been trying are, more or less, those I have calculated for the surviving planets as of today. And, of course, intermediate radii to make sure that we will be measurably perturbed no matter where those planets actually are. It's just a matter of getting close enough to one of them.'

'If our food lasts,' groaned Ryerson. 'And we have to eat while we finish the web, too. Don't forget that.'

'We're going to have to reorganise our schedules,' said Maclaren thoughtfully. 'Hitherto we've found things to keep us occupied. Now we must wait, and not go crazy waiting.' He grinned. 'I hereby declare the *Southern Cross* dirty-limerick contest open and offer a prize of – '

'Yes,' said Ryerson. 'Great sport. Fun and games, with Chang Sverdlov's frozen corpse listening in!'

Silence clapped down. They heard the air mumble in the ventilators.

'What else can we do with our poor friend?' asked Nakamura softly. 'Send him on a test rocket into the black sun? He deserved better of us. Yes-s-s? Let his own people bury him.'

'Bury a copy of him!' shrieked Ryerson. 'Of all the senseless – '

'Please,' said Nakamura. He tried to smile. 'After all , . . it is no trouble to us, and it will comfort his friends at home, maybe yes? After all, speaking in terms of atoms, we do not even wish to send ourselves back. Only copies.' He laughed.

*'Will you stop that giggling!'*

'Please.' Nakamura pushed himself away, lifting astonished hands. 'Please, if I have offended you, I am so sorry.'

'So sorry! So sorry! Get out of here! Get out, both of you! I've seen more of you than I can stand!'

Nakamura started to leave, still bobbing his head, smiling and hissing in the shaftway. Maclaren launched himself between the other two. He snapped a hand on to either wrist.

'That will do!' They grew suddenly aware, it was

103

shocking, how the eyes turned green in his dark hooked face. His words fell like axes. 'Dave, you're a baby, screaming for mother to come change you. Seiichi, you think it's enough to make polite noises at the rest of the world. If you ever want to see sunlight again, you'll both have to mend your ideas.' He shook them a little. 'Dave, you'll keep yourself clean. Seiichi, you'll dress for dinner and talk with us. Both of you will stop feeling sorry for yourselves and start working to survive. And the next step is to become civilised again. We haven't got the size or the time or the force to beat that star: nothing but manhood. Now go off and start practicing how to be men!'

They said nothing, only stared at him for a few moments and then departed in opposite directions. Maclaren found himself gazing stupidly at his guitar case. *I'd better put that away till it's requested*, he thought. *If ever. I didn't stop to think, my own habits might possibly be hard to live with.*

After a long time: *Seems I'm the captain now, in fact if not in name. But how did it happen? What have I done, what have I got?* Presently, with an inward twisting: *It must be I've less to lose. I can be more objective because I've no wife, no children, no cause, no God. It's easy for a hollow man to remain calm.*

He covered his eyes, as if to deny he floated among a million unpitying stars. But he couldn't hunch up that way for long. Someone might come back, and the captain mustn't be seen afraid.

Not afraid of death. Of life.

# 14

SEEN from a view turret on the observation deck, the planet looked eerily like its parent star which had murdered it. Ryerson crouched in darkness, staring out to darkness. Against strewn constellations there lay a gigantic black outline with wan streaks and edgings of gray. As he watched, Ryerson saw it march across the Milky Way and out of his sight. But it was the *Cross* which moved, he thought, circling her hope in fear.

*I stand on Mount Nebo*, he thought, *and down there is my Promised Land.*

Irrationally – but the months had made them all odd, silent introverts. Trappists because meaningful conversation was too rare and precious to spill without due heed – he reached into his breast pocket. He took forth Tamara's picture and held it close to him. Sometimes he woke up breathing the fragrance of her hair. *Have a look,* he told her. *We found it.* In a heathen adoration: *You are my luck, Tamara. You found it.*

As the black planet came back into sight, monstrously swallowing suns (it was only a thousand or so kilometers away), Ryerson turned his wife's image outward so she could see what they had gained.

'Are you there, Dave?'

Maclaren's voice came from around the cylinder of the living section. It had grown much lower in this time of search. Often you could scarcely hear Maclaren when he spoke. And the New Zealander, once in the best condition of them all, had lately gotten thinner than the other two, until his eyes stared from caves. But then, thought Ryerson, each man aboard had had to come to terms with himself, one way or another, and there had been a price. In his own case, he had paid with youth.

'Coming.' Ryerson pulled himself around the deck, between the instruments. Maclaren was at his little desk, with a clipboard full of scrawled paper in one hand. Nakamura had just joined him. The Saraian had gone wholly behind a mask, more and more a polite unobtrusive robot. Ryerson wondered whether serenity now lay within the man, or the loneliest circle of hell, or both.

'I've got the data pretty well computed,' said Maclaren.

Ryerson and Nakamura waited. There had been curiously little exultation when the planet finally revealed itself. *I,* thought Ryerson, *have become a plodder. Nothing is quite real out here – there is only a succession of motions, in my body and my brain – but I can celebrate no victory, because there is none, until the final and sole victory: Tamara.*

*But I wonder why Terangi and Seiichi didn't cheer?*

Maclaren ruffled through his papers. 'It has a smaller mass and radium than Earth,' he said, 'but a considerably higher density suggesting it's mostly nickel-iron. No satellite, of course. And, even though the surface gravity it a bit more than Earth's, no atmosphere. Seems to be bare rock down there . . . or metal, I imagine. Solid, anyhow.'

'How large was it once?' murmured Nakamura.

Maclaren shrugged. 'That would be pure guesswork,' he said. 'I don't know which planet of the original system this is. One or two of the survivors may have crashed on the primary by now, you see. My personal guess, though, is that it was the 61 Cygni C type – more massive than Jupiter, though of less bulk because of core degeneracy. It had an extremly big orbit. Even so, the supernova boiled away all its hydrogen and probably

106

some of the heavier elements too. But that took time, and the planet still had this much mass left when the star decayed into a white dwarf. Of course, with the pressure of the outer layers removed, the core reverted to normal density, which must have been a pretty spectacular catastrophe in itself. Since then, the residual stellar gases have been making the planet spiral slowly inward, for hundreds of megayears. And now – '

'Now we found it,' said Ryerson. 'With three weeks' food supply to spare.'

'And the germanium still to get,' said Maclaren.

Nakamura drew a breath. His eyes went to the deck 'beneath' his feet. Far aft was a storage compartment which had been left open to the bitterness of space; and a dead man, lashed to a stanchion.

'Had there been four of us,' he said, 'we would have consumed our supplies already and be starving. I am most humbly grateful to Engineer Sverdlov.'

Maclaren's tone was dry. 'He didn't die for that reason.'

'No. But has he given us less, merely because it was an accident?'

They floated a while in stillness. Then Maclaren shook himself and said: 'We're wasting time. This ship was never intended to land on a planet. Since I've already informed you any world we found might very likely use vacuum for sky, and you didn't object, I assume the aircraft can make a landing.'

Nakamura crossed his legs and rested impassively, hands folded on his lap. 'How familiar are you with the standard exploratory technique?' he inquired.

'Not very,' confessed Maclaren. 'I gather that aircraft are preferred for reasons of mass economy.'

'And even more for maneuverability. A nuclear-powered vessel, using wings and turbojets, can rise high into an atmosphere, above the worst air resistance, without having to expand the reaction mass of a rocket. Likewise it can land more easily and safely in the first

107

place. The aircraft which we carry, dismantled, are intended to leave their orbiting mother ship with a short rocket burst, slip into the atmosphere of a new planet, and descend. The return is more difficult, of course, but they get into the stratosphere before applying the non-ionic rocket drive. This in turn takes them into space proper, where their ion accelerators will work. Naturally, the cabins being sealed, any kind of atmosphere will serve them.

'Now, this is for exploration purposes. But these auxiliary craft are also capable of landing on rockets alone. When the time had come to establish a beam-relay station, some airless, lifeless satellite is chosen, to avoid the necessity of quarantine. The craft shuttle back and forth, carrying the ship's dismantled transceiver. This is reassembled on the surface. Thereby the satellite's own mass becomes available to the matter bank, and any amount of material can be reconstructed according to the signals from the home station. The first things sent through are usually the parts for a much larger transceiver station, which can handle many tons of mass at a time.'

'Well, good,' said Maclaren. 'That was more or less what I thought. Let's land and – oh, oh.'

Ryerson felt a smile tugging his lips, though it was not a happy one. 'You see?' he murmured.

Maclaren regarded him closely. 'You don't seem too discouraged,' he said. 'There must be an answer.'

Ryerson nodded. 'I've already spoken with Seiichi about it, while you were busy determining the exact characteristics of the planet. It's not going to be fun, but – Well, let him tell you.'

Maclaren said slowly: 'I had hoped, it was at least possible, that any planet we found would have a surviving satellite, small enough to land the whole ship on, or lay alongside if you want to consider it that way. It would have been the best thing for us. But I'm sure now that this lump has no companion of any kind. So we'll have to get our germanium down there.'

'Which we could also have done, had we been fortunate enough to locate the planet sooner,' Nakamura told him. 'We can take aircraft down to the surface even now. But we would have to transship all the mining and separating equipment, establish a working space and an airdome – It is too much work for three men to do before our three weeks of supplies are eaten up; and then the actual mining would still remain.'

Maclaren nodded. 'I should have thought of this myself,' he said. 'I wonder how sane and sensible we are – how can we measure rationality, when we are all the human race we know for tens of light-years? – Well. So I didn't think and you didn't talk. Nevertheless, I gather there's a way out of our dilemma.'

'Yes,' the pilot. 'A riskful way, but any other is certain death. We can take the ship down, and use her for our ready-made workshop and airdome.'

'The *Cross*? But – well, of course the gravitation here is no problem to her, nor the magnetism now that the drive is shielded . . . but we can't make a tail landing, we'd crumple and the web, and – hell's clanging bells, she can't land at all! She's not designed for it! Not maneuverable enough, why, it takes half an hour just to swing her clear around on gyros.'

Nakamura said calmly, 'I have made calculations for some time now, preparing for this eventuality. There was nothing we could do before knowing what we would actually find, but I do have some plans drawn up. We have six knocked-down auxiliary craft. Yes? It will not take long to assemble their non-ionic rocket drives, which are very simple devices, clamp these to the outside hull, and run their control systems through the ship's console. I think if we all work hard we can have it assembled, tested, and functioning in two or three days. Each pair of rockets should be so mounted as to form a couple which will rotate the ship around one of the three orthogonal space axes. No? Thus the spaceship will become most highly responsive to piloting. Furthermore, we shall cut up the aircraft hulls, as well as whatever else we may need and can spare for this purpose, such as interior fittings. From this, we shall construct a tripod enclosing and protecting the stern assembly. It will be clumsy and unbalanced, of course – but I trust my poor maneuverings can compensate for that – and it will be comparatively weak – but with the help of radar and our powerful ion-blast, the ship can be landed very gently.'

'Hm-m.' Maclaren rubbed his chin. His eyes flickered between the other two faces. 'It shouldn't be hard to fix those rocket motors in place, as you say. But a tripod more than a hundred meters long, for a thing as massive as this ship – I don't know. If nothing else, how about the servos for it?'

'Please.' Nakamura waved his words aside. 'I realise we have not time to do this properly. My plan does not envision anything with self-adjusting legs. A simple, rigid structure must suffice. We can use the radar to select a nearly level landing place.'

'All places are, down there,' said Maclaren. 'That iron was boiling once, and nothing has weathered it since. Of course, there are doubtless minor irregularities, which would topple us on our tripod – with a thousand tons of mass to hit the ground!'

Nakamura's eyes drooped. 'It will be necessary for me to react quickly,' he said. 'That is the risk we take.'

When the ship was prepared, they met once on the observation deck, to put on their spacesuits. The hull might be cracked in landing. Maclaren and Ryerson would be down at the engine controls, Nakamura in the pilot's turret, strapped into acceleration harness with only their hands left free.

Nakamura's gaze sought Maclaren's. 'We may not meet again,' he said.

'Possible,' said Maclaren.

110

The small, compact body held steady, but Nakamura's face thawed. He had suddenly, after all the time which was gone, taken on an expression; and it was gentle.

'Since this may be my last chance,' he said, 'I would like to thank you.'

'Whatever for?'

'I am not afraid any more.'

'Don't thank me,' said Maclaren, embarrassed. 'Something like that, a chap does for himself, y'know.'

'You earned me the time for it, at least.' Nakamura made a weightless bow. '*Sensei*, give me your blessing.'

Maclaren said, with a degree of bewilderment: 'Look here, everybody else has had more skill, contributed more, than I. I've told you a few things about the star and the planet, but you – Dave, at last – could have figured it out with slightly more difficulty. I'd never have known how to reconstruct a drive or a web, though; and I'd never be able to land this ship.'

'I was not speaking of material survival,' said Nakamura. A smile played over his mouth, 'Still, do you remember how disorganised and noisy we were at first, and how we have grown so quiet since and work together so well? It is your doing. The highest interhuman art is to make it possible for others to use *their* arts.' Then, seriously, 'The next stage of achievement, though, lies within a man. You have taught me. Knowingly or not, Teranga-san, you have taught me. I would give much to be sure you will . . . have the chance . . . to teach yourself.'

Ryerson appeared from the lockers. 'Here they are,' he said. 'Tin suits all around.'

Maclaren donned his armor and went aft. *I wonder how much Seiichi knows. Does he know that I've stopped making a fuss about things, that I didn't exult when we found this planet, not from stoicism but merely because I have been afraid to hope?*

*I wouldn't even know what to hope for. All this struggle, just to get back to Earth and resume having fun?*

*No, that's too grotesque.*

'We should have issued the day's chow before going down,' said Ryerson. 'Might not be in any shape to eat it at the other end.'

'Who's got an appetite under present circumstances?' said Maclaren. 'So postponing dinner is one way of stretching out the rations a few more hours.'

'Seventeen days' worth, now.'

'We can keep going, foodless, for a while longer.'

'We'll have to,' said Ryerson. He wet his lips. 'We won't mine our metal, and gasify it, and separate out the fractional per cent of germanium, and make those transistors, and tune the circuits, in any seventeen days.'

Maclaren grimaced. 'Starvation, or the canned willy we've been afflicted with. Frankly, I don't think there's much difference.'

Hastily, he grinned at Ryerson, so the boy would know it for a jest. Grumbling was not allowed any more; they didn't dare. And the positive side of conversation, the dreaming aloud of 'when we get home', had long since worn thin. Dinner-table conversation had been a ritual they needed for a while, but in a sense they had outgrown it. Now a man was driven into his own soul. *And that's what Seiichi meant,* thought Maclaren. *Only, I haven't found anything in myself. Or, no. I have. But I don't know what. It's too dark to see.*

He strapped himself in and began checking instruments.

'Pilot to engine room. Read off!'

'Engine room to pilot. Plus voltage clear. Minus voltage clear. Mercury flow standard . . . '

The ship came to life.

And she moved down. Her blast slowed her in orbit, she spiraled, a featureless planet of black steel called her to itself. The path was cautious. There must be allowance for rotation; there must not be too quick a change of velocity, lest the ponderous sphere go wobbling out of control. Again and again the auxiliary motors blasted, spinning her, guiding her. The ion-drive was not loud, but the rockets roared on the hull like hammers.

And down. And down.

Only afterward, reconstructing confused memories, did Maclaren know what had happened; and he was never altogether sure. The *Cross* backed on to an iron plain. Her tripod touched, on one foot, on two. The surface was not quite level. She began to topple. Nakamura lifted her with a skill that blended main drive and auxiliaries into one smooth surge – such skill as only an utterly relaxed man could achieve, responding to the immense shifting forces as a part thereof. He rose a few hundred meters, changed position relative to the ground, and tried again. The tripod struck on two points once more. The ship toppled again. The third leg went off a small buff, no more than a congealed ripple in the iron. It hit ground hard enough to buckle.

Nakamura raised ship barely in time. For an instant he poised in the sky in a single leg of flame, keeping his balance with snorts of rocket thrust. The bottom of the *Cross*' stern assembly was not many meters above ground.

Suddenly he killed the ion drive. Even as the ship fell, he spun her clear around on the rotator jets. The *Cross* struck nose first. The pilot's turret smashed, the bow caved in, automatic bulkheads slammed shut to save the air that whistled out. That was a great mass, and it struck hard. The sphere was crushed flat for meters aft of the bow. With her drive and her unharmed transceiver web aimed at the sky, the ship rested like Columbus' egg.

And the stars glittered down upon her.

Afterward Maclaren wondered: Nakamura might well have decided days beforehand that he would probably never be able to land any other way. Or he might have considered that his rations would last two men an extra week. Or perhaps, simply, he found his dark bride.

# 15

THE planet spun quickly about its axis, once in less than ten hours. There went never a day across its iron plains, but hunger and the stars counted time. There was no wind, no rain, no sea, but a man's radio hissed with the thin dry talk of the stars.

When he stood at the pit's edge and looked upward, Maclaren saw the sky sharp and black and of an absolute cold. It had a somehow three-dimensional effect; theory said all those crowding suns, blue-white or frosty gold or pale heatless red, were alike at optical infinity, but the mind sensed remoteness beyond remoteness, and whimpered. Nor was the ground underfoot a comfort, for it was almost as dark, starlit vision reached a few meters and was gulped down. A chopped-off Milky Way and a rising constellation (the one Maclaren had privately named Risus, the Sneer) told him that a horizon existed, but his animal instinct did not believe it.

He sighed, slapped a glare filter across his faceplate, and began cutting. The atomic hydrogen torch was lurid enough to look upon, but it jostled the stars out of his eyes. He cut rapidly, ten-kilo slabs which he kicked down into the pit so they wouldn't fuse tight again. The hole itself had originally been blasted, but the *Cross* didn't carry enough explosive for him to mine all his ore that way.

Ore, he reflected, was a joke. How would two men on foot prospect a sterilised world sealed into vacuum a hundred million years ago? And there would have been little point in it. This planet had boiled once, at

114

least on the surface; and even the metallic core had been heated and churned, quite probably to melting, when crushed atoms expanded to normal dimensions. The entire globe must be nearly uniform, one alloy lump. You took any piece, crushed it, gasified it, ionized it, put it through the electromagnetic isotope separator, and drew forth as much (or, rather, as minutely little) germanium as any other piece would have given you. From the known rate of extraction by such methods you could calculate when you would have four kilograms. The date lay weeks away.

Maclaren finished cutting, shut off his torch and hung it on its generator, and climbed into the bucket of the crane at the pit's edge. His flashbeam threw puddles of light on its walls as he was lowered. At the bottom he moved painfully about, loaded the bucket, and rode back to the surface. A small electric truck waited, he spilled the bucket into its box. And then it was to do again, and still again, until he had a full load.

Thank God and her dead designers, the *Cross* was well equipped for work on airless surfaces, she carried machines to dig and build and transport. But, of course, she had to. It was her main purpose, to establish a new transceiver station on a new moon; everything else could then come straight from the Solar System.

It had been her purpose.

Before heaven, it still was.

Maclaren climbed wearily on to the truck seat. He and his spacesuit had fourth again their Earth-weight here. His headlights picked out a line of paint leading toward the ship. It had been necessary to blast the pit some distance away, for fear of what ground vibrations might do to the web or the isotope separator. But then a trail had to be blazed, for nature had given no landmarks for guide, this ground was as bare as a skull.

Existence was like lead in Maclaren's bones.

After a while he made out the *Cross*, a flattened sphere crowned with a skeleton and the Orion nebula. It was no fun having everything upside down within her; a whole day had gone merely to reinstall the essential items. Well, Seiichi, you did what seemed best, and your broken body lies honored with Chang Sverdlov's, on the wide plains of iron.

Floodlights glared under the ship. Ryerson was just finishing the previous load, reducing stone to pebbles and thence to dust. Good timing. Maclaren halted his truck and climbed down. Ryerson turned toward him. The undiffused glow reached through his faceplate and picked a sunken, bearded face out of night, little more than nose and cheekbone and bristling jaw. In his unhuman armor, beneath that cavernous sky, he might have been a troll. *Or I might,* thought Maclaren. *Humanity is far from us. We have stopped bathing, shaving, dressing, cooking . . . pretending; we work till our brains go blank, and then work some more, and crawl up the ladder into the ship for a few hours' uneasy sleep, and are awakened by the clock, and fool our shriveled bellies with a liter of tea, and put a lump of food in our mouths and go out. For our time has grown thin.*

'Hello, Nibelung,' said Ryerson.

Maclaren started. 'Are you getting to be a telepath?'

'It's possible,' said Ryerson. His voice had become a harsh whisper. His glance searched darkness. 'Anything is possible here.'

'After we put this load through,' said Maclaren, evading the other thought, 'we'd better move the slag out of the ship. That ninety-nine-plus per cent of material we don't use piles up fast.'

'M-hm.' Ryerson clumped heavily to the truck and began unloading. 'And then out once more, cutting and loading and grinding and – merciful God, but I'm tired! Do you really imagine we can keep on doing heavy manual work like this, after the last food has been eaten?'

'We'll have to,' said Maclaren. 'And, of course, there is always – ' He picked up a rock. Dizziness whirled

116

through him. He dropped the stone and sank to his knees on the ground.

'Terangi!' Ryerson's voice seemed to come from some Delphic deep, through mists. 'Terangi, what's wrong?'

'Nothing,' mumbled Maclaren. He pushed at the other man's groping arms. 'Lea' me be . . . all right in a minute . . . ' He relaxed against the stiffness of armor and let his weakness go through him in tides.

After a while, some strength returned. He looked up. Ryerson was just feeding the last rocks into the crusher. The machine ate them with a growl that Maclaren felt through the planet and his body. It vibrated his teeth together.

'I'm sorry, Dave,' he said.

' 'S all right. You should go up and bunk for a while.'

'Just a spell. Maybe we shouldn't have cut our rations as short as we have.'

'You do seem to've been losing weight even faster than me,' said Ryerson. 'Maybe you ought to have an extra ration.'

'Nah. It's metabolic inefficiency, brought on by well-spent years of wine, women, and off-key song.'

Ryerson sat down beside him. 'I'm a bit short of breath myself. Let's both take a break while the stuff goes through the crusher.'

'Well,' said Maclaren, 'if your tailbone insulators can stand it, I suppose mine can.'

They remained in silence for a while. The machine rumbled in their flesh and the stars muttered in their heads.

'How long do you think it will take to prepare the web?' asked Maclaren. 'I mean, what's your latest estimate?'

'Hitherto I've underestimated the time for everything,' said Ryerson. 'Now, I just don't know. First we'll have to get our germanium. Then, to make the units . . . I don't know. Two weeks, three? And then, once all the circuits are functioning, they'll have to be tuned. Mostly

117

by guesswork, since I don't really know the critical constants. That will take $x$ time, depending on how lucky we are.'

'We'll open the last can of food soon,' said Maclaren. In itself it was a totally useless reminder, but it was leading up to something they had both avoided.

Ryerson continued to squirm: 'They say tobacco helps kill appetite.'

'It does,' said Maclaren, 'but I smoked the last butts months ago. Now I've even lost the addiction. Though of course I'll happily rebuild same the moment we strike Earth.'

'When we come home . . . ' Ryerson's voice drifted off like a murmur in sleep. 'We haven't talked about our plans for a long time.'

'It got to be too predictable, what every man would say.'

'Yes. But is it now? I mean, do you still want to take that sailboat cruise around Earth, with . . . er . . . a female crew and a cargo of champagne?'

'I don't know,' said Maclaren, faintly surprised to realise it. 'I hadn't thought. . . . Do you remember once in space, we talked about our respective sailing experiences, and you told me the sea is the most inhuman thing on our planet?'

'Mm-m-m – yes. Of course, my sea was the North Atlantic. You might have had different impressions.'

'I did. Still, Dave, it has stuck in my mind, and I see now you are right. Any ocean is, is too – big, old, blind for us – too beautiful.' He sought the million suns of the Milky Way. 'Even this black ocean we're wrecked in.'

'That's odd,' said Ryerson. 'I thought it was your influence making me think more and more of the sea as a – not a friend, I suppose. But hope and life and, oh, I don't know. I only know I'd like to take that cruise with you.'

'By all means,' said Maclaren. 'I didn't mean I'd become afraid of the water, just that I've looked a little deeper into it. Maybe into everything. Hard to tell, but I've had a feeling now and then, out here, of what Seiichi used to call insight.'

One does learn something in space,' agreed Ryerson. 'I began to, myself, once I'd decided that God hadn't cast me out here and God wasn't going to bring me back, it wasn't His part – Oh, about that cruise. I'd want to take my wife, but she'd understand about your, uh, companions.'

'Surely,' said Maclaren. 'I'd expect that. You've told me so much about her, I feel like a family friend.' *I feel as if I loved her.*

'Come around and be avuncular when we've settled – Damn, I forgot the quarantine. Well, come see our home on Rama in thirty years!'

Maclaren: *No, no, I am being foolish. The sky has crushed me back toward child, because she has gallant eyes and hair like a dark flower, it does not mean she is the one possible woman to fulfill that need I have tried for most of my life to drown out. It is only that she is the first woman since my mother's death whom I realise is a human being.*

*And for that, Tamara, I have been slipping three-fourths of my ration back into the common share, so your man may innocently take half of that for his. It is little enough I can do, to repay what you who I never saw gave to me.*

'Terangi! You're all right, aren't you?'

'Oh. Oh, yes, of course.' Maclaren blinked at the other armored shape, shadowy beside him. 'Sorry, old chap. My mind wandered off on some or other daisy-plucking expedition.'

'It's an odd thing,' said Ryerson, 'I find myself think-ing more and more frivolously. As this cruise of yours, for instance. I really mean to join you, if you're still willing, and we'll take that champagne along and stop at every sunny island and loaf about and have a hell of a good time. I wouldn't have expected this . . . what

119

has happened . . . to change me in that direction. Would you?'

'Why, no,' said Maclaren. 'Uh, I thought actually you – '

'I know. Because God seemed to be scourging me, I believed that whole creation must lie under His wrath. And yet, well, I have been on the other side of Dooms-day. Here, in nightmare land. And somehow, oh, I don't know, but the same God who killed that nova saw equally fit to . . . to make wine for the wedding at Cana.'

Maclaren wondered if the boy would regret so much self-revelation later. Perhaps not if it had been mutual. So he answered with care, 'Oddly enough, or maybe not so oddly, my thinking has drifted in the other direction. I could never see any real reason to stay alive, except that it was more fun than being dead. Now I couldn't begin to list all the reasons. To raise kids into the world, and learn something about the universe, and not com-promise with some crowned bastard's version of justice, and . . . I'm afraid I'm not a convert or anything. I still see the same blind cosmos governed by the same blind laws. But suddenly it matters. It matters terribly, and means something. What, I haven't figured out yet. I probably never will. But I have a reason for living, or for dying if need be. Maybe that's the whole purpose of life: purpose itself. I can't say. But I expect to enjoy the world a lot more.'

Ryerson said in a thoughtful tone, 'I believe we've learned to take life seriously. Both of us.'

The grinder chuted its last dust into the receptacle. The gasifier was inboard; and the cold, not far from absolute zero, was penetrating the suit insulators. Ryerson got up. Shadows lapped his feet. 'Of course,' he said, his voice suddenly cracked, 'that doesn't help us a great deal if we starve to death out here.'

Maclaren rose with him. The floodlamps ridged both their faces against the huge hollow dark. Maclaren caught

Ryerson's eyes with his own. For a moment they struggled, not moving under the constellations, but sweat sprang out upon Ryerson's forehead.

'You realise,' said Maclaren, 'that we actually can eat for quite a while longer. I'd say, at a guess, two more months.'

'No,' whispered Ryerson. 'No, I won't.'

'You will,' Maclaren told him.

He stood there another minute, to make certain of his victory, which he meant as a gift to Tamara. Then he turned on his heel and walked over to the machine. 'Come on,' he said, 'let's get to work.'

# 16

MACLAREN woke up of himself. For a moment he did not remember where he was. He had been in some place of trees, where water flashed bright beneath a hill. Someone had been with him, but her name and face would not come back. There was a lingering warmth on his lips.

He blinked at the table fastened to the ceiling. He was lying on a mattress –

Yes. The *Southern Cross*, a chilly knowledge. But why had he wakened early? Sleep was the last hiding place left to him and Dave. They stood watch and watch at the web controls, and came back to their upside-down bunkroom and ate sleep. Life had shrunken to that.

Maclaren yawned and rolled over. The alarm clock caught his eye. Had the stupid thing stopped? He looked at the second hand for a while, decided that it was indeed moving. But then he had slept for – holy shark-toothed sea gods – for thirteen hours!

He sat up with a gasp. Bloodlessness went through his head. He clung to his blankets and waited for strength to come back. How long a time had it been, while his tissues consumed themselves for lack of all other nourishment? He had stopped counting hours. But the ribs and joints stuck out on him so he sometimes listened for a rattle when he walked. Had it been a month? At least it was a time spent inboard, with little physical exertion; that fact alone had kept him alive.

Slowly, like a sick creature, he climbed to his feet. If Dave hadn't called him, Dave might have passed out, or died, or proven to have been only a starving man's whim. *With a host of furious fancies* – Maclaren shambled across to the shaftway. The transceiver rooms were aft of the gyros, they had been meant to be 'down' with respect to the observation deck whenever there was acceleration and now they were up above. Fortunately, the ship had been designed in the knowledge she would be in free fall most of her life. Maclaren gripped a rung with both hands. *I could use a little free fall right now,* he reflected through the dizziness. He put one foot on the next rung, used that leg and both hands to pull the next foot up beside it; now, repeat; once more; one for Father and one for Mother and one for Nurse and one for the cat and so it goes until here we are, shaking with exhaustion.

Ryerson sat at the control panel outside the receiving and transmitting chambers. It has been necessary to spot-weld a chair, with attached ladder, to the wall and, of course, learn how to operate an upside-down control panel. The face that turned toward Maclaren was bleached and hairy and caved-in; but the voice seemed almost cheerful, 'So you're awake.'

'The alarm didn't call me,' said Maclaren. He panted for air. 'Why didn't you come rouse me?'

'Because I turned off the alarm in the first place.'

'What?' Maclaren sat down on what had been the ceiling and stared upward.

'You'll fall apart if you don't get more rest,' said Ryerson. 'You've been in worse shape than me for weeks, even before the . . . the food gave out. I can sit here and twiddle knobs without having to break off every eight hours.'

'Well, maybe.' Maclaren felt too tired to argue.

'Any luck?' he asked after a while.

'Not yet. I'm trying a new sequence now. Don't worry, we're bound to hit resonance soon.'

Maclaren considered the problem for a while. Lately his mind seemed to have lost as much ability to hold things as his fingers. Painfully, he reconstructed the theory and practice of gravitic mattercasting. Everything followed with simple logic from the fact that it was possible at all.

The signals necessarily used a pulse code, with amplitude and duration as the variables; there were tricky ways to include a little more information through the number of pulses per millisecond, if you set an upper limit to the duration of each. It all took place so rapidly that engineers could speak in wave terms without too gross an approximation. Each transceiver identified itself by a 'carrier' pattern, of which the actual mattercasting signal was a modulation. The process only took place if contact had been established, that is, if the transmitter was emitting the carrier pattern of a functioning receiver: the 'resonance' or 'awareness' effect which beat the inverse-square law, a development of Einstein's great truth that the entire cosmos is shaped by what momentarily happens to each of its material parts.

The 'caster itself, by the very act of scanning, generated the signals which recreated the object transmitted. But first the 'caster must be tuned in on the desired receiving station. The manual aboard ship gave the call pattern of every established transceiver: but, naturally, gave it in terms of the standardised and tested web originally built into the ship. Thus, to reach Sol, the book said, blend its pattern with that of Rashid's Star, the initial relay station in this particular case. Your signal will be automatically bucked on, through several worlds, till it reaches Earth's Moon. Here are the respective voltages, oscillator frequencies, etc., involved; add them up and use the resultant.

Ryerson's handmade web was not standardised. He could put a known pattern into it, electronically, but the gravitics would emit an unknown one, the call signal of a station not to be built for the next thousand years. He lacked instruments to measure the relationship, so he could not recalculate the appropriate settings. It was cut and try, with a literal infinity of choices and only a few jackleg estimates to rule out some of the possibilities.

Maclaren sighed. A long time had passed while he sat thinking. Or so his watch claimed. He hadn't noticed it go by, himself.

'You know something, Dave?' he said.

'Hm?' Ryerson turned a knob, slid a vernier one notch, and punched along a row of buttons.

'We are out on the far edge of no place. I forget how far to the nearest station, but a devil of a long ways. This haywire rig of ours may not have the power to reach it.'

'I knew that all the time,' said Ryerson. He slapped the main switch. Needles wavered on dials, oscilloscope tracings glowed elfhill green, it whined in the air. 'I think our apparatus is husky enough, though. Remember, this ship has left Sol farther behind than any other ever did. They knew she would – a straight-line course would just naturally outrun the three-dimensional expansion of our territory – so they built the transceiver with capacity to spare. Even in its present battered state, it might reach Sol directly. If conditions were just right.'

'Think we will? That would be fun.'

Ryerson shrugged. 'I doubt it, frankly. Just on a statistical basis. There are so many other stations by now – *Hey!*'

Maclaren found himself on his feet, shaking. 'What is it?' he got out. 'What is it? For the love of heaven, Dave, what is it?'

Ryerson's mouth opened and closed, but no sounds emerged. He pointed with one bony arm. It shook.

Below him (it was meant to be above, like a star) a light glowered red.

'Contact,' said Maclaren.

The word echoed through his skull as if spoken by a creator, across a universe still black and empty.

Ryerson began to weep, silently, his lips working.

'Tamara,' he said. 'Tamara, I'm coming home.'

Maclaren thought: *If Chang and Seiichi had been by me now, what a high and proud moment.*

'Go on, Terangi,' chattered Ryerson. His hands shook so he could not touch the controls. 'Go on through.'

Maclaren did not really understand it. Not yet. It was too swift a breaking. But the wariness of a race which had evolved among snakes and war spoke for him: 'Wait, Dave. Wait a minute. Just to be certain. Put a signal through. A teletype, I mean; we've no voice microphone, have we? You can do it right at that keyboard.'

'What for?' screamed Ryerson. 'What for? If you won't go through, I will!'

'Just wait, is all.' Suddenly Maclaren was begging. All the craziness of months between stars that burned his eyes woke up; he felt in a dim way that man must live under conditions and walk in awe, but this is one of the prides of being a man. He raised powerless hands and cried – it was not much above a whisper – 'There could be some distortion, you know. Accidents do happen, once in a great while, and this web was made by hand, half of it from memory. . . . Send a message. Ask for a test transmission back to us. It won't take long and . . . My God, Dave, what kind of thing could you send home to Tamara if the signal was wrong?'

Ryerson's chin quivered in its beard, but he punched the typer keys with hard angry strokes. Maclaren sat back down, breathing quickly and shallowly. So it was to become real after all. So he would again walk beneath the tall summer clouds of Earth.

*No*, he thought. *I never will. Terangi Maclaren died in an orbit around the black sun, and on the steel planet where there is always winter. The I that am may go home, but never the I that was.*

Ryerson bent over so he could look into the screen which gave him an image of the receiving chamber.

Maclaren waited. A long while passed.

'Nothing,' said Ryerson. 'They haven't sent a thing.'

Maclaren could still not talk.

'A colonial station, of course,' said Ryerson. 'Probably one of the outpost jobs with two men for a staff . . . or, Lord, another spaceship. Yes, that's likeliest, we're in touch with an interstellar. Only one man on watch and – '

'And there should be a bell to call him, shouldn't there?' asked Maclaren, very slowly.

'You know how they get on the long haul,' said Ryerson. He smote his chair arm with a fist that was all knobs. 'The man is sleeping too hard to hear a thing. Or – '

'Wait,' said Maclaren. 'We've waited long enough. We can afford a few more minutes, to make certain.'

Ryerson blazed at him, as if he were an enemy. 'Wait? Wait, by jumping hell! No!'

He set the control timer for transmission in five minutes and crept from his seat and down the ladder. Under the soiled tunic, he seemed all spidery arms and legs, and one yellow shock of hair.

Maclaren stood up again and stumbled toward him. 'No,' he croaked. 'Listen, I realise how you feel, but I realise it's space lunacy too, and I forbid you, I forbid – '

Ryerson smiled. 'How do you propose to stop me?' he asked.

'I – but can't you wait, wait and see and – '

'Look here,' said Ryerson. 'Let's assume there is a freak in the signal. A test transmission comes through. At best, the standard object is merely distorted . . . at worst, it won't be recreated at all, and we'll get an explosion. The second case will destroy us. In the first case, we haven't time to do much more work. I doubt if I could climb around on the web outside any more. I know damn well you couldn't, my friend! We've no choice but to go through. Now!'

'If it's a ship at the other end, and you cause an

explosion,' whispered Maclaren, 'you've murdered one more man.'

Drearily, as if from far away, he recognised the hardness which congealed the other face. Hope had made David Ryerson young again. 'It won't blow up,' said the boy, and was wholly unable to imagine such a happening.

'Well . . . probably not . . . but there's still the chance of molecular distortion or – ' Maclaren sighed. Almost experimentally, he pushed at Ryerson's chest. Nothing happened; he was so much more starved that he could not move the lank body before him.

'All right,' said Maclaren. 'You win. I'll go through.'

Ryerson shook his head. 'No, you don't,' he answered. 'I changed my mind.' With a lilt of laughter: 'I stand behind my own work, Terangi!'

'No, wait! Let me – I mean – think of your wife, at least – please – '

'I'll see you there,' cried Ryerson. The blue glance which he threw over his shoulder was warm. He opened the transmitter room door, went through, it clashed shut upon him. Maclaren wrestled weakly with the knob. No use, it had an automatic lock.

*Which of us is the fool? I will never be certain, whatever may come of this. The chances are all for him, of course . . . in human terms, reckoned from what we know . . . but could he not learn with me how big this universe is, and how full of darkness?*

Maclaren stumbled back toward the ladder to the chair. He would gain wrath, but a few more minutes, by climbing up and turning off the controls. And in those minutes, the strangely, terrifyingly negligent operator at the other end might read the teletype message and send a test object. And then Ryerson would know. Both of them would know. Maclaren put his feet on the rungs. He had only two meters to climb. But his hands would not lift him. His legs began to shake. He was halfway to the panel when its main switch clicked down and the transmission engine skirled.

He crept on up. *Now I know what it means to be old,* he thought.

His heart fluttered feebly and wildly as he got into the chair. For a while he could not see the vision screens, through the night the spumed in his head. Then his universe steadied a little. The transmitter room was quite empty. The red light still showed contact. So at least there had been no destruction wrought in the receiving place. Except maybe on Dave; it didn't take much molecular warping to kill a man. *But I am being timid in my weakness. I should not be afraid to die. Least of all to die. So let me also go on through and be done.*

He reached for the timer. His watch caught his eye. Half an hour since Dave left? Already? Had it taken half an hour for him to creep this far and think a few sentences? But surely Dave would have roused even the sleepiest operator. They should have sent a teletype to the *Cross*: 'Come on, Terangi. Come on home with me.' What was wrong?

Maclaren stared at the blank walls enclosing him. Here he could not see the stars, but he knew how they crowded the outside sky, and he had begun to understand, really understand what an illusion that was and how hideously lonely each of those suns dwelt.

*One thing more I have learned, in this last moment,* he thought. *I know what it is to need mercy.*

Decision came. He set the timer for ten minutes – his progress to the transmitter room would be very slow – and started down the ladder.

A bell buzzed.

His heart sprang. He crawled back, feeling dimly that there were tears on his own face now, and stared into the screen.

A being stood in the receiving chamber. It wore some kind of armor, so he could not make out the shape very well, but though it stood on two legs the shape was not a man's. Through a transparent bubble of a helmet, where the air within bore a yellowish tinge, Maclaren saw its face. Not fish or frog or mammal, it was so other a face that his mind would not wholly register it. Afterward he recalled only blurred features, there were tendrils and great red eyes.

Strangely, beyond reason, even in that first look he read compassion on the face.

The creature bore David Ryerson's body in its arms.

# 17

WHERE Sunda Straits lay beneath rain (but sunlight
came through to walk upon the water) the land fell steep.
It was altogether green, in a million subtle hues, jungle
and plantation and rice paddy, it burned with green
leaves. White mists wreathed the peak of a volcano, and
was it thunder across wind or did the mountain talk in
sleep?

Terangi Maclaren set his aircar down on brown-and-
silver water and taxied toward the Sumatra shore. Each
day he regained flesh and strength, but the effort of
dodging praus and pontoon houses and submarines still
tired him. When his guide pointed: 'There, tuan,' he cut
the engines and glided in with a sigh.

'Are you certain?' he asked, for there were many such
huts of thatch and salvaged plastic along this coast. It was
a wet world here, crowding brown folk who spent half
their cheerful existences in the water, divers, deckhands,
contracting their labor to the sea ranches but always
returning home, poverty, illiteracy, and somehow more
life and hope than the Citadel bore.

'Yes, tuan. Everyone knows of her. She is not like the
rest, and she holds herself apart. It marks her out.'

Maclaren decided the Malay was probably right. Tamara Suwito Ryerson could not have vanished completely
into the anonymous proletariat of Earth. If she still
planned to emigrate, she must at least leave a mailing
address with the Authority. Maclaren had come to Indo-
nesia quickly enough, but there his search widened, for a
hundred people used the same P.O. in New Djakarta and

their homes lay outside the cosmos of house numbers and phone directories. He had needed time and money to find this dwelling.

He drove up on to the shore. 'Stay here,' he ordered his guide, and stepped out. The quick tropic rain poured over his tunic and his skin. It was the first rain he had felt since . . . how long? It tasted of morning.

She came to the door and waited for him. He would have known her from the pictures, but not the grace with which she carried herself. She wore a plain sarong and blouse. The rain filled her crow's-wing hair with small drops and the light struck them and shattered.

'You are Technic Maclaren,' she said. He could scarcely hear her voice, so low did it fall, but her eyes were steady on his. 'Welcome.'

'You have seen me on some newscast?' he inquired, banally, for lack of anything else.

'No. I have only heard. Old Prabang down in the village has a nonvisual set. But who else could you be? Please come in, sir.'

Only later did he realise how she broke propriety. But then, she had declared herself free of Protectorate ways months ago. He found that out when he first tried to contact her at her father-in-law's. The hut, within, was clean, austerely furnished, but a vase of early mutation-roses stood by David's picture.

Maclaren went over to the cradle and looked down at the sleeping infant. 'A son, isn't it?' he asked.

'Yes. He has his father's name.'

Maclaren brushed the baby's cheek. He had never felt anything so soft. 'Hello, Dave,' he said.

Tamara squatted at a tiny brazier and blew up its glow. Maclaren sat down on the floor.

'I would have come sooner,' he said, 'but there was so much else, and they kept me in the hospital –'

'I understand. You are very kind.'

'I . . . have his effects . . . just a few things. And I will arrange the funeral in any way you desire and – ' His

132

voice trailed off. The rain laughed on the thatch.

She dipped water from a jar into a teakettle. 'I gather, then,' she said, 'there was no letter that he wrote?'

'No. Somehow . . . I don't know. For some reason none of us wrote any such thing. Either we would all perish out there, and no one else would come for fifty or a hundred years, or we would get back. We never thought it might be like this, a single man.' Maclaren sighed. 'It's no use trying to foresee the future. It's too big.'

She didn't answer him with her voice.

'But almost the last thing Dave said,' he finished awkwardly, 'was your name. He went in there thinking he would soon be home with you.' Maclaren stared down at his knees. 'He must have – have died quickly. Very quickly.'

'I have not really understood what happened,' she said, kneeling in the graceful Australian style to set out cups. Her tone was flattened by the effort of self-control. 'I mean, the 'cast reports are always so superficial and confused, and the printed journals so technical. There isn't any middle ground any more. That was one reason we were going to leave Earth, you know. Why I still am going to, when our baby has grown just a little bit.'

'I know how you feel,' said Maclaren. 'I feel that way myself.'

She glanced up with a startled flirt of her head that was beautiful to see. 'But you are a technic!' she exclaimed.

'I'm a human being too, my lady. But go on, ask me your question, whatever you were leading up to. I've a favor of my own to ask, but you first.'

'No, what do you want? Please.'

'Nothing very important. I've no claim on you, except the fact that your husband was my friend. I'm thinking of what you might do for his sake. But it will wait. What did you wonder about?'

'Oh. Yes. I know you tuned in the aliens' transceiver and didn't realise it. But – ' Her fists clenched together. She stared through the open door, into the rain and the light, and cried forth: 'It was such a tiny chance! Such a meaningless accident that killed him!'

Maclaren paused until he had all his words chosen. Then he said, as gently as might be: 'It wasn't so wildly improbable. All this time we've known that we couldn't be the only race reaching for the stars. It was absurd to think so; that would have been the senseless unlikelihood. Well, the *Cross* was farther out than men had ever gone before, and the alien spaceship was near the aliens' own limit of expansion. It was also bound for Alpha Crucis. Odd what a sense of kinship that gives me, my brother mariner, with chlorine in his lungs, silicon in his bones, steering by the same lodestar. Contact was certain eventually, as they and we came into range of each other's signals. Your David was the man who first closed the ring. We were trying call patterns we could not measure, running through combinations of variables. Statistically, we were as likely to strike one of their patterns as one of ours.'

The water began to boil. She busied herself with the kettle. The long tresses falling past her face hid whether she was crying or not. Maclaren added for her. 'Do you know, my lady, I think we must have called hundreds of other space-traveling races. We were out of their range, of course, but I'm sure we called them.'

Her voice was muffled: 'What did the aliens think of it?'

'I don't know. In ten years we may begin to talk to them. In a hundred years, perhaps we will understand them. And they us, I hope. Of course, the moment David ... appeared ... they realised what had happened. One of them came through to me. Can you imagine what courage that must have taken? How fine a people your man has given us to know? There was little they could do for me, except test the *Cross'* web and rule out all the call patterns which they use. I kept on trying, after that. In a week I finally raised a human. I went through to his receiver and that's all. Our technicians are now building a new relay station on the black star planet. But they'll leave the *Cross* as she is, and David Ryerson's name will be on her.'

'I thought,' she whispered, still hiding her face, 'that you . . . I mean, the quarantine rules – '

'Oh, yes, the Protectorate tried to invoke them. Anything to delay what is going to happen. But it was useless. Nothing from the aliens' planet could possibly feed on Terrestrial life. That's been established already, by the joint scientific commission; we may not be able to get the idea behind each other's languages yet, but we can measure the same realities! And of course, the aliens know about us. Man just can't hide from the universe. So I was released.' Maclaren accepted the cup she offered him and added wryly: 'To be sure, I'm not exactly welcome at the Citadel any more.'

She raised large eyes to him. He saw how they glimmered. 'Why not?' she asked. 'You must be a hero to – '

'To spacemen, scientists, some colonials, and a few Earthmen glad of an end to stagnation. Not that I deserve their gratitude. There are three dead men who really did all this. But at any rate, my lady, you can foresee what an upheaval is coming. We are suddenly confronted with – Well, see here, the aliens must be spread through at least as large a volume of space as man. And the two races don't use the same kind of planets. By pooling transceiver networks, we've doubled both our territories! No government can impose its will on as many worlds as that.

'But more. There are sciences, technologies, philosophies, religions, arts, insights they have which we never imagined. It cannot be otherwise. And we can offer them ours, of course. How long do you think this narrow little Protectorate and its narrow little minds can survive such

135

an explosion of new thought?' Maclaren leaned forward. He felt it as an upsurge in himself. 'My lady, if you want to live on a frontier world, and give your child a place where it's hard and dangerous and challenging – and everything will be possible for him, if he's big enough – stay on Earth. The next civilisation will begin here on Earth herself.'

Tamara set down her cup. She bent her face into her hands and he saw, helpless, how she wept. 'It may be,' she said to him, 'it may be, I don't know. But why did it have to be David who bought us free? Why did it have to be him? He didn't mean to. He wouldn't have, if he'd known. I'm not a sentimental fool, Maclaren-san, I know he only wanted to come back here. And he died! There's no meaning in it!'

# 18

THE North Atlantic rolled in from the west, gray and green and full of thunder. A wind blew white manes up on the waves. Low to the south gleamed the last autumnal daylight, and clouds massed iron-colored in the north, brewing sleet.

'There,' pointed Tamara. 'That is the place.'

Maclaren pointed his aircar earthward. The sky whistled around him. So Dave had come from here. The island was a grim enough rock, harshly ridged. But Dave had spoken of gorse in summer and heather in fall and lichen of many hues.

The girl caught Maclaren's arm. 'I'm afraid, Terangi,' she whispered. 'I wish you hadn't made me come.'

'It's all we can do for David,' he told her. 'The last thing we'll ever be able to do for him.'

'No.' In the twilight, he saw how her head lifted. 'There's never an end. Not really. His child and mine, waiting, and – At least *we* can put a little sense into life.'

'I don't know whether we do or whether we find what was always there,' he replied. 'Nor do I care greatly. To me, the important thing is that the purpose – order, beauty, spirit, whatever you want to call it – does exist.'

'Here on Earth, yes,' she sighed. 'A flower or a baby. But then three men die beyond the sun, and it so happens the race benefits a little from it, but I keep thinking about all those people who simply die out there. Or come back blind, crippled, broken like dry sticks, with no living soul the better for it. Why? I've asked it and asked it, and there isn't ever an answer, and finally I think that's because there isn't any why to it in the first place.'

Maclaren set the car down on the beach. He was still on the same search, along a different road. He had not come here simply to offer David's father whatever he could: reconciliation, at least, and a chance to see David's child now and then in the years left him. Maclaren had some obscure feeling that an enlightenment might be found on Skula.

Truly enough, he thought, men went to space, as they had gone to sea, and space destroyed them, and still their sons came back. The lure of gain was only a partial answer; spacemen didn't get any richer than sailors had. Love of adventure . . . well, in part, in some men, and yet by and large the conquerors of distance had never been romantics, they were workaday folk who lived and died among sober realities. When you asked a man what took him out to the black star, he would say he had gone under orders, or that he was getting paid, or that he was curious about it, or any of a hundred reasons. Which might all be true. And yet was any of them the truth?

And why, Maclaren wondered, did man, the race, spend youth and blood and treasure and all high hopes upon the sea and the stars? Was it only the outcome of meaningless forces – economics, social pressure, maladjustment, myth, whatever you labeled it – a set of chance-created vectors with the sardonic resultant that man broke himself trying to satisfy needs which could have been more easily and sanely filled at home?

*If I could get a better answer than that,* thought Maclaren, *I could give it to Tamara. And to myself. And then we could bury our dead.*

He helped her out of the car and they walked up a path toward the ancient-looking cottage. Light spilled from its windows into a dusk heavy with surf. But they had not quite reached it when the door opened and a man's big form was outlined.

'Is that you, Technic Maclaren?' he called.

'Yes. Captain Magnus Ryerson?' Maclaren stepped ahead of Tamara and bowed. 'I took the liberty, sir, of bringing a guest with me whom I did not mention when I called.'

'I can guess,' said the tall man. 'It's all right, lass. Come in and welcome.'

As she passed over the uneven floor to a chair, Tamara brushed Maclaren and took the opportunity to whisper, 'How old he's grown, all at once!'

Magnus Ryerson shut the door again. His hands, ropy with veins, shook a little. He leaned heavily on a cane as he crossed the room and poked up the fire. 'Be seated,' he said to Maclaren. 'When I knew you were coming, I ordered some whisky from the mainland. I hope it's a good make. I drink not, you see, but be free to do so yourself.'

Maclaren looked at the bottle. He didn't recognise the brand. 'Thank you,' he said, 'that's a special favorite of mine.'

'You've eaten?' asked the old man anxiously.

'Yes, thank you, sir.' Maclaren accepted a glass. Ryerson limped over the floor to give Tamara one.

'Can you stay the night? I've some extra beds in the garret, from when the fisher lads would come by. They come no more, there's no reason for it now, but I've kept the beds.'

Maclaren traded a look with Tamara. 'We would be honored,' he said.

Magnus Ryerson shuffled to the hob, took the teakettle, poured himself a cup and raised it. 'Your health.' He sat down in a worn chair by the fire. His hands touched a leather-bound book lying on its arm.

There was silence for a while, except that they could all hear the waves boom down on the strand.

Maclaren said finally: 'I . . . we, I mean . . . we came to – to offer our sympathy. And if there was anything I

139

could tell you . . . I was there, you know.'

'Aye. You're kind.' Ryerson groped after a pipe. 'It is my understanding he conducted himself well.'

'Yes. Of course he did.'

'Then that's what matters. I'll think of a few questions later, if you give me time. But that was the only important one.'

Maclaren looked around the room. Through its shadows he saw pilot's manuals on the shelves, stones and skins and gods brought from beyond the sky; he saw the Sirian binary like twin hells upon darkness, but they were very beautiful. He offered: 'Your son was in your own tradition.'

'Better, I hope,' said the old man. 'There would be little sense to existence, did boys have no chance to be more than their fathers.'

Tamara stood up. 'But that's what there isn't!' she cried all at once. 'There's no sense! There's just dying and dying and dying – what for? – so that we can walk on still another planet, learn still another fact – what have we gained? What have we really done? And why? In your own God's name, what did we do once that He sends our men out there now?'

She clamped her hands together. They heard how the breath rasped in her. She said at last, 'I'm sorry,' and sat back down. Her fingers twisted blind until Maclaren took them.

Magnus Ryerson looked up. And his eyes were not old. He let the surf snarl on the rocks of his home for a while, and then he answered her, ' *"For that is our doom and our pride."* '

'What?' She started. 'Oh. In English. Terangi, he means – ' She said it in Interhuman.

Maclaren sat quite still.

Ryerson opened his book. 'They have forgotten Kipling now,' he said. 'One day they will remember. For no people live long, who offer their young men naught but fatness and security. Tamara, lass, let your son hear this

140

one day. It is his song too, he is human.'

The words were unknown to Maclaren, but he listened and thought that in some dark way he understood.

' *"We have fed our sea for a thousand years*
*And she calls us, still unfed,*
*Though there's never a wave of all her waves*
*But marks our English dead:*
*We have strawed our best to the weed's unrest,*
*To the shark and the sheering gull.*
*If blood be the price of admiralty,*
*Lord God, we ha' paid in full!"* '

When Ryerson had finished, Maclaren stood up, folded his hands and bowed. '*Sensei*,' he said, 'give me your blessing.'

'What?' The other man leaned back into shadows, and now he was again entirely old. You could scarcely hear him under the waves outside. 'You've naught to thank me for, lad.'

'No, you gave me much,' said Maclaren. 'You have told me why men go, and it isn't for nothing. It is because they are men.'

*Two men and one woman in a desperate battle*
*to win a Galactic empire – or destroy it!*

POUL ANDERSON
# The Rebel Worlds

**The barbarians in their long ships**
**waiting at the edge of the Galaxy ...**

... waited for the ancient Terran Empire to fall, while
two struggled to save it: ex-Admiral McCormac, forced to
rebel against a corrupt Emperor, and Starship Commander
Flandry, the brilliant young officer who served the
Imperium even as she scorned it.
Trapped between them was the woman they both loved, but
couldn't share: the beautiful Kathryn –whose single word
could decide the fate of a billion suns.

JOHN WYNDHAM
# Stowaway to Mars

An international prize of £1,000,000 was being offered
to the first man to complete an interplanetary journey,
and Dale Curtance, a millionaire adventurer,
characteristically emerges as the British entrant. With a
hand-picked crew he blasted off from Salisbury Plain in
the spaceship GLORIA MUNDI, destination—the planet
Mars. Once free of the Earth's atmosphere, they discover
a stowaway, a woman. Her extraordinary story helps
prepare them for the dangers they encounter on the
Red Planet, and the fantastic world that exists there.

'A classic, ripe with wit and eloquence and a cascade of inventiveness. Alpha plus' BRIAN ALDISS

*From the author of*
*SLAUGHTERHOUSE 5*

KURT VONNEGUT Jr.

# The Sirens of Titan

**TITAN – one of the moons of Saturn, and a place of delight**

Among the inhabitants – **Winston Runfoord,** a space traveller caught up in chronosynclastic infundibulum (one of the hazards of intruding into space-time); **Malachi Constant,** the richest and luckiest man on earth, now in exile, and what price his riches now; and **Sato,** a visitor from Tralfamadore, a planet in another galaxy, bearing a message from one rim of the universe to the other. Some visitor, some message . . .

'Kurt Vonnegut's best seller . . . a work of great scope and staggering originality'

BOOKS AND BOOKMEN

'Wildly funny invention' SUNDAY TIMES

'A really good one' PUNCH

# TRIP THE LIGHT FANTASTIC
# WITH CORONET

*All these books are available at your bookshop or newsagent, or can be ordered direct from the publisher. Just tick the titles you want and fill in the form below.*

---

CORONET BOOKS, P.O. Box 11, Falmouth, Cornwall.

Please send cheque or postal order. No currency, and allow the following for postage and packing:

1 book – 7p per copy, 2-4 books – 5p per copy, 5-8 books – 4p per copy, 9-15 books – 2½p per copy, 16-30 books – 2p per copy in U.K., 7p per copy overseas.

Name..........................................................

Address.......................................................

..............................................................